"What sort of game are you playing?"

Meredith demanded as she swung around to confront him.

Tom raised his shoulders in feigned innocence. "No game, Mrs. Blake. Just because I won't let you malign me in the local rag, doesn't mean that I can't accept a dinner invitation without an ulterior motive."

"I don't know how you can accept their hospitality, considering what you plan to do. I couldn't, in your place."

Unexpectedly, he reached out to grasp her wrist in a gentle, yet iron, grip. "That's your problem, lady, not mine. You're the one who decided to start up an old folks' home without a licence. I'm surprised no one has questioned your motives. I know what rent I'm charging *you*, but I'd be interested to learn how much you're charging *them*."

Catherine Spencer suggests she turned to romance-fiction writing to keep from meddling in the love lives of her five daughters and two sons. The idea was that she would keep herself busy manipulating the characters in her novels instead. This, she says, has made everyone happy. In addition to writing novels, Catherine Spencer also teaches school in British Columbia, Canada.

Books by Catherine Spencer

HARLEQUIN PRESENTS
910—A LASTING KIND OF LOVE

WINTER ROSES
Catherine Spencer

Harlequin Books

TORONTO • NEW YORK • LONDON
AMSTERDAM • PARIS • SYDNEY • HAMBURG
STOCKHOLM • ATHENS • TOKYO • MILAN

Original hardcover edition published in 1990
by Mills & Boon Limited

ISBN 0-373-03138-6

Harlequin Romance first edition July 1991

With love to Sean, my son and housebuilder

WINTER ROSES

CHAPTER ONE

ALARM had Meredith sitting on the edge of her chair and wiping her palms discreetly on her skirt. 'Not renew the lease?' she said sharply, forgetting that Reginald Swabey did not have the stamina to deal with aggressive or irate young women. 'What do you mean, *not renew the lease*?'

From his gilt frame on the wall behind Mr Swabey, Ernest Fitch, 1846-1930, late founder of Fitch, Fitch, Crawford and Swabey, Riverbridge's first law firm, glared disapprovingly through his pince-nez. No doubt in his day and age members of the opposite sex who liked to consider themselves ladies knew better than to raise their voices at gentlemen, or question the infallibility of masculine judgement. Times having changed, however, Meredith merely glared back.

Mr Swabey cleared his throat nervously. 'Well—er—Mrs Blake...Meredith—er—what I mean is that—er—the owner does not wish to renew the...er—the lease.'

'Why not?'

'Why not...?' He shuffled through the papers on his desk. Sunlight, slanting through the tall, narrow windows, turned his thinning white hair to silver beneath which his scalp glowed pinkly. 'I'm afraid Mr Whitney did not choose to—er—disclose his reasons.'

'What *did* he disclose, Mr Swabey?'

'Oh, dear!' Mr Swabey removed his glasses and polished them anxiously. 'I'm afraid he's served you with two months' notice to find—er—other premises.'

Two months in which to find a house large enough to accommodate eight adults and two cats? Meredith's thoughts and heart raced frantically, but she maintained her surface control. 'Impossible, Mr Swabey,' she declared firmly. 'Tell Mr Whitney *six* months and not a day less.'

Two months, six months, a year—what did it matter? She'd never find another suitable house in Riverbridge.

'Oh, dear!' Mr Swabey blinked and popped his glasses back on his nose. 'I don't know...Mr Whitney seemed quite emphatic that, when he arrived in town——'

'I'm quite emphatic, too, Mr Swabey. Please convey my terms and if Mr Whitney chooses to discuss the matter with me personally I assume he knows where he can reach me.'

'Oh, dear me, yes.' Mr Swabey almost tittered. 'It's his house, after all.'

'One would hardly think so,' Meredith replied tartly, 'considering the disgraceful state of disrepair in which he keeps it.' She rose and extended her hand across the desk, noting how cautiously the lawyer touched her fingertips in return. 'Good day, Mr Swabey. It was a pleasure to see you again.'

Spine erect, she marched out of the office and past the four desks lined up in the reception area. Four pairs of startled eyes followed her as the staccato rap of her high heels on the marble floor drowned out the clatter of typewriters. Ignoring the disapproving glances, Meredith swept out of the building and waited until she reached the street before allowing herself to wilt.

It was still a beautiful late June day. To all appearances, nothing much had changed since she'd entered this same building a scant half-hour earlier, yet a man she'd never seen or spoken to had made a decision that threatened to turn eight lives upside-down, and it seemed that there was nothing she could do to stop him.

Where would her tenants go, if they were turned out of the Whitney house? And how was she going to break the news to them that they were about to be evicted from the only place they could call home—in two months' time, if Mr Whitney had his way?

The shade of the maples that lined the main street dappled the pavement with shifting patterns. A light breeze, perfumed with the scent of carnations blooming in front of the court-house across the square, lifted the hair that clung damply to Meredith's forehead. A class of six-year-olds trooped towards the wrought-iron gates of the park with their teacher, their voices pitched high with excitement at the prospect of spending Friday afternoon outside in the sunshine instead of in a stuffy classroom.

Yes, indeed, Meredith thought, watching them. The park was delightful when the paths were bordered with flowers, and the old wooden benches felt like warm satin in the heat. But it was a different story in the middle of winter when snow covered the ground, and the wind howled through the naked branches of the trees and whipped the duck pond into a froth of angry waves. Then, a person needed to be able to come home to a roaring fire and a hot meal, and to know that, when night fell, there was a cosy bed waiting.

Damn Thomas Patrick Whitney! If he thought she was about to lie down and let him walk all over her and her 'family', he was in for a surprise. Maybe she couldn't prevent him from carrying out his intentions, but she could and would make sure he didn't escape public embarrassment in the process.

A grim smile touched her mouth. She could see it now: 'Absentee Landlord Whitney Evicts Elderly Tenants'. A fine thing that would be for the revered family name—spread all over the front page of the local newspaper! The Whitney ancestors would roll over in their graves at the disgrace.

Joshua Hartley, editor of the *Riverbridge Times*, narrowed his eyes in uncustomary malice when he heard her request. 'Print your story? Meredith, girl, I'll do more than that. I'll give you front-page coverage in the weekend edition. We'll show that miserable big-city slicker. Never did give a rap about anybody in this town. Would have sold his own mother down the river if he could have got away with it, and she a God-fearing, law-abiding woman past the age where she ever expected to be raising a boy like that, poor soul.'

Meredith was a little startled. The Joshua Hartley she knew was a soft-spoken, tolerant sort of man. 'I didn't realise you knew him so well, Joshua.'

He scowled. 'Everyone knew him. He was an affront to decent society.' He rubbed his hands again. 'I never thought I'd have the chance to get even with him.'

'I just want you to print the facts,' Meredith insisted, rather taken aback at the vehemence of the editor's reaction. Maybe the two men had been rivals in school or something; maybe they'd courted the same girl when they were young, and Joshua had come away the loser. 'He hasn't actually done anything wrong—yet.'

'Give him time,' Joshua predicted gloomily, hauling his bulk out from behind his desk and walking her to the door. He patted her on the shoulder. 'Andrew would be proud of you, if he knew what you'd taken on. It's not often someone your age bothers with the old folks unless she has to. Once our memory starts to go and we begin forgetting our table manners, it's a sight easier to shove us off into some seedy old institution and forget all the years we put in raising families. I don't know where your bunch would be if you hadn't taken them in and made a home for them.'

Meredith smiled. 'Let's hope Mr Whitney comes to see things in the same light.'

'Hmph! Seeing and caring are two different things. Unless he's changed, of course, and from the sound of it he hasn't, except to grow worse.'

Meredith took the long way home through the park. She needed time to think, to plan how she was going to break the news to the rest of the family. She could hardly wait until they read about their plight in Sunday morning's paper. They were too old to sustain such a shock. The problem was, she hadn't the faintest idea how she was going to soften the blow.

Florence had made cauliflower soup for dinner. It was one of Meredith's favourites, but she had no appetite for it, nor for the new potatoes from the garden, nor the roast chicken that accompanied them. Instead, she found herself looking at the familiar faces around the table and trying to envisage what her life would be like without them.

It was over three years since she'd found Eleanor wandering in the park late one November evening. Sleet had soaked through the thin coat the old lady had been wearing and turned her shoes to sodden cardboard. That had been reason enough to take her home for the night, but it was Eleanor's lost air, of a person her age being adrift in an uncaring world, that had prompted Meredith to keep her, even though she probably could have found Eleanor a place in a shelter.

It was also what had saved Meredith's sanity. Eleanor had come on the scene at a time when Meredith had thought there was nothing left in the world that really mattered. Andrew had been dead just eight months, and the numbness had worn off to expose a grief that she thought would last for the rest of a life that threatened to be too long and empty to be endured.

People had told her that the secret to recovery was to take small steps, one day at a time. Well, Eleanor had been the first small step, and from there things had begun to improve. Prudence and Henry had come to her for help next, and that was when the search for a larger house had begun.

At first, Meredith had been against the Whitney place. It was too big, too draughty, too run-down. But it was cheap, which had been the deciding factor, and, as soon became apparent, there was no lack of tenants to fill the rooms. Without ever having planned it, Meredith had found herself running a home for senior citizens, and loving it.

Before she'd married Andrew and come to live in Riverbridge, she had been a social worker in Vancouver and had thought that, after what she'd seen there, nothing could shock her. To discover that there were homeless elderly people sleeping on park benches—bag ladies, they were called in the city—in a town so small that hardly anyone called anyone else 'Mr' had horrified her.

Riverbridge was so correct on the surface. No one littered the streets, no one drove too fast, no one picked the flowers outside the court-house or stole the money from the fountain in the square, and just about everyone went to church on Sundays. It was such a proper little place, in fact, that people still remembered the time years ago when Thomas Patrick Whitney had been a rude, unmanageable boy, so scarce had the species become among later generations.

What would it take to appeal to the man's better nature now—assuming he had one? Not the fact that Bill had coaxed the garden back to something approaching past glory, nor that Dolores suffered from angina but wasn't ready to settle for a nursing home. Nor the fact that Florence was a fabulous cook who made sure they all ate nutritious meals three times a day; nor that, despite her patrician features and blue-rinsed hair, Lucille was as lost and afraid of being alone as Eleanor, for whom this was the first real home she'd known in her seventy-odd years. And certainly not the fact that Henry and Prudence, who were so much in love, couldn't afford to get married and lose their survivors' pensions, which meant that if they applied for a place in the government-run retirement complex on the edge of town they'd have to take two separate rooms. Thomas Whitney wouldn't care. He probably didn't believe in love.

'You're very quiet tonight. Is there something wrong, Meredith?'

Lucille's question caught her off guard, and Meredith looked up to find herself the object of considerable curiosity from the others around the table.

'You haven't touched your chicken,' Florence accused. 'And you didn't finish your soup. Don't you feel well?'

Meredith, having decided there was no escaping what she had to do, had opened her mouth to speak when Eleanor gave a little shriek and pointed to the window. 'There's someone outside! I saw a face looking in at us!'

In the general commotion, Meredith's lack of appetite was forgotten. With Henry and Bill leading the way, everyone trooped through the front door and out to the long, covered veranda.

'Are you sure you saw someone?' Dolores asked, peering into the dusk. As far as any of them could determine, the garden was empty and none of the shadows under the trees moved to indicate someone might be lurking there.

Eleanor was trembling. 'There was a face,' she insisted.

Lucille snorted disparagingly. 'Oh, really, Eleanor, you try my patience! If you're not getting lost, you're living in the past half the time. And now you're seeing things and we're all letting a perfectly good dinner grow cold while we look for something that's not there. Well, I'll have none——'

'Was it a man or a woman you saw, Eleanor?' Meredith asked gently. She knew that Lucille could intimidate Eleanor into silence when she adopted that sort of attitude and, although it was hard to believe a Peeping Tom would dare to set foot within miles of Riverbridge, if there had indeed been someone peering through the windows, Meredith certainly wanted to find out who, and why.

'I couldn't tell,' Eleanor whispered. 'I just saw the face, I really did, Meredith.'

Bill, who'd gone down the front steps to inspect the flower-bed under the veranda, overheard her. 'Yes, you did, Eleanor. I raked this garden this afternoon, and there are fresh footprints in it, plain as day.' He drew in an irate breath and pointed. 'And whoever he was, the devil broke down my American Beauty rose.'

'Well, he's gone now,' Henry consoled them, 'so I suppose we might as well go back inside. It was probably just some youngster playing a prank, but I think you and I should check all the locks before we turn in tonight, Bill, just to be on the safe side.'

Prudence drew closer to Henry at that, and Eleanor let out a little whimper. Meredith didn't have the heart to upset them further by telling them about Thomas Whitney's decision to evict them. It could wait until the morning. Even though the weekend edition of the newspaper went on sale on Saturday evening, they didn't get their copy delivered until Sunday morning, so she had a little time on her side.

But the next day they woke up to more sunshine, and once breakfast was over everyone seemed to have plans that took them out of the house. Bill worked in the garden. Henry went to buy supplies for making more wine and took Prudence with him. Lucille always had her hair done on Saturday afternoon, and liked to treat herself to lunch at the Riverbridge Hotel first, so she left right after she'd watered the house plants. Dolores and Florence took the ferry across the river to the farmers' market and phoned to say they wouldn't be back before dinner, and Eleanor wanted to sit in the park and watch the children playing.

Left pretty much to herself, Meredith prepared a cold meat salad for lunch and looked over her accounts. After she and Bill had eaten, she washed her hair and sat outside to let it dry in the sun, glad that it required so little care. She'd always wished she'd been born blonde or black-haired, or a flaming redhead. There was something so dramatic about that sort of colouring, but she supposed that being blessed with natural curls compensated for also being stuck with basic brown. She might not have the most memorable face, but at least she'd never have to worry about being caught with her hair in rollers.

The back garden was blissfully peaceful. Wistaria and clematis climbed over the veranda railing, and the cottonwoods at the bottom end of the property sighed in the light breeze. Meredith sighed, too. She hadn't slept very well last night and a tension headache threatened now, brought on by her inability to resolve her family's predicament. She'd never been much good at dealing with uncertainty, especially not where the future was concerned, and there was no use deluding herself. It was going to be terribly hard to find a house big enough for all of them, and absolutely impossible to find one that would compare with the Whitney house.

Siamantha, the purer bred of the two cats that also shared the house, jumped up and kneaded herself to comfort on Meredith's lap, while her soul mate, Albert, wound himself lovingly between Meredith's ankles. 'It isn't fair,' Meredith murmured, leaning back in her chair and closing her eyes. The cats purred agreement, and half a block away a lawnmower droned in sympathy.

He'd been back in town no more than two hours, and already he was wondering what masochistic streak had prompted him to visit the place one last time. Had he really expected anything to have changed for the better during his unlamented absence?

Pulling aside the layers of curtains and draperies at his hotel-room window, Tom looked down on the main street of his birthplace with about as much affection as any other man would have viewed a penitentiary. Which, when he stopped to think about it, was a pretty fair description of how Riverbridge had always affected him: stifling, confining, judgemental, and punitive. And oh, so bloody righteous! He wasn't a man given to using particularly bad language, but there was something about this town and the people living in it that made him want to stand in the square below and swear at the top of his voice, just for the perverse pleasure of outraging the citizens.

Instead, he turned back to the room behind him and scowled. Apparently as opposed to change as the locals, the décor was unrelentingly Victorian. He found the faded red upholstery and ornate walnut furniture depressing and claustrophobic, and wondered again why he'd forsaken the comforts of his airy Toronto apartment to make this pilgrimage to a town that was no more welcoming towards him now than it had been when he was seventeen.

Irritably, he collected his room key and wallet and made for the door. It was only three o'clock, but he was about to invite further condemnation by parking himself in the bar downstairs and ordering a beer, in full view of anyone loitering in the lobby. Darby Bradford had recognised him and looked as affronted as if he'd been forced to admit a felon to the premises when Tom had checked in. No doubt it would make the man's day to be able to broadcast that the Whitney boy had fallen prey to the evils of alcohol along with his many other sins.

Tomorrow he'd list the house and the two river-front lots with an estate agent, then head back east on Monday. The remainder of his summer vacation he'd spend scuba-diving in the Caribbean, or windsurfing in Kauai. Anything was better than exposing himself to the hostility of a bunch of small-minded, small-town people who preferred to focus on their memories of a smart-mouthed, immature kid rather than the fact that he'd grown up and made something of himself. Being proven wrong always did sit ill with them.

He drew in an extended breath and shook his head, unable to believe that he even cared. What did local opinion matter as long as he knew who he was?

He was halfway through his second beer when someone spoke his name. 'By God, they were right, it is you! I'd recognise those shoulders anywhere. Tom Whitney, it's good to see you again.'

Tom spun around on his stool, a grin inching over his features. 'Mike Upman, what in the world are you doing here? The last I heard, you were setting the newspaper industry on its ear in Vancouver.'

'I couldn't stay away, pal.' Mike's answering grin took on a sheepish cast. 'Came back and married Lorna Gray, my high-school sweetheart.'

Tom groaned. 'Correct me if I'm wrong, but weren't you one of the founding members of the Single and Staying That Way Fraternity? I suppose the next thing you'll be telling me is you've got the requisite two and a half children.'

'Four, as a matter of fact.'

Tom whistled and inspected his old schoolfriend more closely. 'Amazingly enough, it seems to suit you. I take it you've got a pretty good marriage?'

'The best.'

'That's a nice change from what I usually hear in my business.' Tom signalled the bartender and raised his eyebrows at Mike. 'Let's celebrate. What'll you have?'

'A beer, thanks, but it'll have to be fast. I've got a few things to tie up at the *Times* before we wrap up for the week.'

Tom didn't try to hide his scorn. 'You're working for that rag?'

'It's a living, Tom, and to be fair, it's improved since Josh Hartley took over as editor.'

'Josh——? Not *the* Josh Hartley we both remember so well from our misspent youth? The one who held me responsible for a tragedy I knew nothing about and couldn't have prevented even if I had?'

Mike lifted his glass in a toast. 'The very same.'

'Good lord,' Tom muttered, 'does nothing ever change in this backwater swamp? He must be in his dotage by now.'

'Hardly. As a matter of fact, he remembers you only too well, which shouldn't come as any surprise, and which is also why I'm here now. When I heard you'd checked into town, I thought you'd want to know about this right away.' Mike looked around uneasily and slid a rolled-up copy of the weekend edition across the bar. 'You're rattling a lot of chains with your plans for the old house, Tom.'

He'd been slouching comfortably over the bar, but something about Mike's tone had Tom sitting suddenly upright. He reached for the newspaper, unfolded it at the front page, and felt a slow rage start to burn inside. But he hadn't become the successful divorce lawyer he was without perfecting a few skills, and keeping an impassive countenance under pressure was one of them. When he finally spoke, his voice was smooth as silk, and if Mike had ever had an occasion to witness Tom at his lethal best in court he'd have recognised the danger signal. 'It seems the widow Blake is bent on a witch hunt, Michael, my friend, and your boss is running dangerously close to a libel suit.'

Mike ran a finger inside his collar. 'Look, Tom, you and I go back a long way, and I'm putting my own job on the line bringing you this copy before the early edition hits the news-stands, but I had to let you know what you're up against, and I've got to tell you, you're going to stir up a lot of old ill feeling if you persist with this. Isn't there some other way to go about it?'

'There might have been,' Tom replied in that same dangerous tone, 'if the good widow hadn't been so hell-bent on malice. I hope she's as prepared to lose as she is to fight.'

'Listen.' Mike shifted uneasily on his stool and leaned forward confidentially. 'Apart from the fact that there are other people involved—old people, Tom; they could be our folks, our grandparents, some of them——'

'Not mine,' Tom cut in. 'According to local lore, I wasn't born to my folks. I was a noxious weed that sprang up in an otherwise orderly garden, and refused to go away.'

Mike sighed. 'What I'm trying to tell you, buddy, is that if you go after Meredith Blake you're going to have the whole town on your case—again! She's sort of sacred around here. She was married to Andrew Blake.'

Andrew Blake...the name evoked images of chalkboards and test tubes, of a thin, academic face, stooped shoulders, and a slightly hoarse voice. Tom shrugged indifferently. 'That's her business, but right now she's meddling in my affairs and I don't intend to let her get away with it.'

'I don't know why you want to make such a big deal out of it,' Mike complained.

Tom pushed himself away from the bar and clapped his old friend on the shoulder. 'That's why you're a newspaper man and I'm a lawyer, pal. It's a question of infringement of civil liberties, namely mine.'

'Where are you going?'

'To pay a certain widow a visit, what else?'

Ignoring Mike's protests, Tom signed his bar tab and strode through the hotel lobby to the front entrance, stopping briefly to hand in his key at the desk. Darby Bradford, who'd been the desk clerk for as long as anyone could remember, was no more disposed to be charming in senility than he had been in middle age. He said not a word but the look in his eyes spoke volumes, condemning Tom for past offences and sins yet to be committed.

Glowering, Tom left the revolving door spinning like a top behind him. The whole town could be spoiling for a fight for all he cared. The way he was feeling right now, it would be just fine with him.

CHAPTER TWO

MEREDITH couldn't have been dreaming because she wasn't really asleep, yet neither was she aware of the intruder until Siamantha sank sharp claws into the soft flesh of her thighs and yowled plaintively. At the same instant, Meredith sensed a shadow looming over her, and felt little goosebumps break out over her sun-warmed skin.

Looking up, she found her gaze drawn to the bluest, most compelling pair of eyes she'd ever seen. 'Who are you?' she asked, too startled to be afraid.

'Tom Whitney,' the man replied, and took his time looking her over. She suddenly felt very conscious of the fact that she was wearing skimpy shorts and a rather abbreviated top.

Then the name sank home and she sprang to her feet, tumbling Siamantha down on the grass. 'But you can't be!'

He raised one eyebrow and almost smiled. 'Why not?'

Because you're young, she wanted to reply, and I had you figured to be old and miserable, not to mention ugly. 'What are you doing prowling around the back garden this way?' she asked instead.

He acknowledged the question with a shrug and nodded towards the house. 'I didn't bother to ring the bell,' he said. 'There's an old man asleep in a rocking-chair on the front veranda and it seemed a shame to disturb his nap. Is your mother home?'

Meredith paused in the act of tugging her shorts down to cover a bit more of her thighs and shot him a suspicious glance. 'My mother?'

'Mrs Blake, the landlady who also happens to be my tenant.'

Meredith was in no mood to find him either funny or charming. She had planned exactly how she was going to conduct her interview with Thomas Whitney if he ever showed his face, but she hadn't planned on his taking her by surprise like this. She felt at enough of a disadvantage without having to cope with his misplaced attempts to find comic relief in a situation that was anything but amusing for the people she cared about. 'Is that supposed to be a joke?' she snapped.

'Not that I'm aware of,' he replied, bending down to scoop Siamantha into his arms.

'Don't try to pick her up,' Meredith warned hastily. 'She doesn't like...men...'

But the cat was settling into the crook of his arm and narrowing her eyes to turquoise slits of pleasure as his other hand caressed the fur along her back. Thomas Whitney smiled. 'She likes me,' he murmured complacently, as though female adulation was his to command at will.

Meredith couldn't help herself. 'Then I suggest you make the most of her company, because if I have my way she's the only admirer you'll find around here.'

He turned those vivid eyes on her again, assessing her with such close attention to detail that she blushed. 'Well, she's certainly not the only one with claws,' he remarked drily. 'Did your mother teach you to be so nasty, or is it something you learned all by yourself?'

I learned *everything* by myself, she wanted to shout. My mother wasn't around to teach me because she was still a child herself when I was born, and I never stayed in one home long enough to learn anything from a foster-mother—except that the only person I could really count on was myself.

'Perhaps I should introduce myself,' she said coldly. 'I am Meredith Blake, Mr Whitney, and I wish I could say how pleased I am to meet you after all this time.'

If nothing else, she had the pleasure of knowing she'd caught him off guard. His hand stilled and Siamantha's eyes blinked open in reproach. His, however, narrowed perceptibly, leaving Meredith with the uneasy feeling that her victory was likely to be both short-lived and solitary.

'In that case, Mrs Blake, we have a few things to set straight.'

'Not at this precise moment, Mr Whitney.' She wasn't about to do battle dressed like this, with him brazenly looking his fill. He was exactly the sort of adversary who would use the opportunity to his advantage. 'It isn't a convenient time. You should have phoned and made an appointment.'

Depositing the cat back on the lawn, he unfolded the paper tucked under his arm and snapped it open at the front page. 'And given you time to manufacture a reason to justify this? I hardly think so, Mrs Blake.'

Horrified, Meredith made a grab for the newspaper. 'Give that to me before someone else sees it!'

He held it up beyond her reach, his smile openly derisive. 'If you don't want your opinions made public, madam, then I suggest you don't confide in journalists.'

'I'm not worried about that,' she said sharply. 'I just hadn't expected to have to explain anything before tomorrow.'

'Well, you should be worried,' he replied, 'because my reaction is going to be the same regardless. Start packing, Mrs Blake, and tell your residents to do likewise.' He took a step closer to the back veranda. 'Or shall I tell them for you?'

'Don't you dare!' Spinning around, she raced up the steps as though to barricade the entrance to the house. 'We have to talk about this first.'

'It isn't a convenient time, remember?'

Meredith sighed explosively. 'Give me ten minutes. Please! You can wait out here, or on the veranda if you'd rather.'

'Make it fast,' he suggested firmly, and brushed past her to settle himself on the porch swing. The sound of it creaking under his weight followed her all the way through the hall and up the stairs.

Her thoughts raced in time with her fingers as she stripped off the shorts and halter top and tossed them on her bed. She needed a shower and couldn't afford the time to take one, not with him sitting downstairs like a bomb waiting to go off. She wanted to be cool and composed in her dealings with him, and cursed the fine skin that betrayed her by slashing her cheeks pink with agitation. She knew his type of woman: sleek, tall, rail-slender and untouchably sophisticated. The sort who could demolish a man with a look; the sort who conveyed amusement and disdain with the same cool smile. The sort of person *she* was not. The only way she was going to get the better of him was to outwit him, and, from all she'd seen, he'd be a formidable opponent.

Buttoned at last into a white cotton jumpsuit Dolores had made for her, Meredith shoved her feet into sandals at the same time that she reached for her brush. Her hair had dried long ago, and popped into springy curls as she ran the bristles through it. Almost at the door, she turned back and picked up a tube of pale lip-gloss, ran it quickly over her mouth to give her lips a touch of colour, and wished she could as easily eliminate the fire in her cheeks.

She was halfway down the stairs before she realised that the swing had stopped creaking and that there were voices coming from the kitchen. Florence and Dolores were home, and so were Prudence and Henry. And not only had they awakened Bill, they'd also discovered Tom Whitney. She couldn't hear the words, but she recognised his voice, several tones deeper than the other men's, mingling with everyone else's.

They all turned to look at her when she appeared in the doorway. 'We have a guest,' Prudence chirped happily. 'Did you know, Meredith?'

'Of course she did, precious,' Henry beamed. 'See how pretty she looks?'

Meredith's eyes swung from Tom Whitney to the others, and back to Tom Whitney again. He leaned easily against the kitchen counter, his hands in his pockets, and with a little sigh of gratitude Meredith noticed that there was no sign of the newspaper.

'You will stay for dinner, Tom?' Florence indicated the bags she and Dolores had brought back
from the farmers' market. 'We've got enough here
to feed an army, and I'm sure you'd rather eat a
home-cooked meal than sit alone in the hotel
dining-room——'

'Mr Whitney,' Meredith interrupted, 'is here on
business, Florence. I don't think he can spare the
time.'

'I can spare the time,' Tom Whitney drawled,
rolling his gaze appreciatively over her trouser-suit,
'especially if the hotel still serves meatballs on a
Saturday night.'

Henry let out a bellow of laughter. 'It does, son,
and they haven't improved over the years.'

Stay for dinner? Tom? *Son*? Meredith closed her
eyes briefly, only to find, when she opened them
again, that Tom Whitney was watching her with
unveiled amusement. 'I really would prefer to get
down to business,' she insisted. 'Perhaps you could
stay for dinner some other night, if you still feel
welcome once you've finished what you started out
to do.'

'I feel welcome now,' he replied blandly, 'and I
hate to turn down a home-cooked meal.'

'That's settled, then,' Florence beamed, and
shooed him towards where Meredith still stood in
the doorway. 'You two go and talk business, while
Dolores and I fix dinner. Prudence, love, will you
set the table?'

'I'll go down to the cellar and look out a couple
of bottles of wine,' Henry offered. 'What are you
planning to serve, Florence?'

'Fresh trout and green beans. They were a bargain at the market. And fresh strawberries for after.'

Henry scratched his chin consideringly. 'Then the white Bordeaux,' he decided. 'I think that will do very well, with perhaps a bottle of Gewürztraminer to have with the strawberries.'

Tom Whitney was grinning from ear to ear. Meredith could have slapped him. 'Outside!' she snapped, tossing her head in the direction of the back door.

He followed her docilely enough as she marched down the path to the bottom of the garden. She wanted to be well out of earshot of anyone in the house because, although she seldom lost her temper, she had a feeling this was one time when she just might not be able to hang on to her control.

The sun had sunk behind the cottonwoods, slanting between the branches to spotlight a butterfly hovering above a bed of scarlet dahlias. Overhead, the sky had assumed a soft and hazy blue that promised more good weather for tomorrow, and, somewhere in the lilac bushes, birds chirped softly. It was a shame to have to spoil so idyllic a scene, but better here than inside the house.

'Exactly what sort of game are you playing?' Meredith demanded, swinging around to confront him.

He raised his shoulders in feigned innocence. 'No game, Mrs Blake. Just because I won't let you malign me in the local rag, it doesn't mean I can't accept a dinner invitation without an ulterior motive.'

'I don't know how you can accept their hospitality, considering what you plan to do. I couldn't, in your place.'

Unexpectedly, he reached out to grasp her wrist, imprisoning it in a gentle iron grip when she tried to wrench it free. 'That's your problem, lady, not mine. You're the one who decided to start up an old folks' home without a licence. I'm surprised no one's seen fit to question *your* motives. I know what rent I'm charging *you*, but I'd be interested to learn how much you're charging *them*.'

Affronted, Meredith glared at him. 'Those people in there are my friends—more than that, they're my family!—and their pensions are all the money they have coming in. How dare you suggest I'd cheat them of their income?'

'And how dare you suggest that I'd go out of my way to make any unexpected announcement while I'm a guest in their home?'

'Because that's the sort of person you are,' she shot back. 'I've heard all about you.'

'I see my reputation has preceded me,' he said on an exaggerated sigh. 'Why does that surprise me, I wonder?'

Meredith would have none of that. 'If you want to feel sorry for someone, I suggest you save your pity for those poor people in there who are shortly to find themselves homeless, thanks to you.'

He dropped her wrist as though he'd suddenly found holding it a rather unpleasant experience. 'And of course you don't expect me to feel a shred of compassion.'

'Not in the least,' she flared.

He gave her a long, level stare. 'Then I must make sure I don't disappoint you,' he said.

Stepping carefully around her, he began strolling back towards the house, leaving Meredith feeling unaccountably ashamed.

Lucille was at her most gracious during dinner. 'This china belonged to my mother, Mr Whitney. I don't normally offer it for general use, but tonight is something of a special occasion. It's Meissen, you know, and no longer obtainable.'

Thomas Patrick Whitney knew all the right moves, Meredith thought sourly. He ran an experimental finger over the rim of his dinner plate and pursed his lips in a silent whistle. 'Very fine and delicate, Mrs Delong. And very generous of you to allow us the pleasure of using it.'

Lucille smiled and patted her newly rinsed hair.

'It's what's served up on it that counts,' Bill declared. 'Lovely piece of fish, Florence. Cooked to a turn.'

'William,' Lucille confided, leaning towards their guest, 'is a peasant, but he means well.'

'This is an excellent wine,' Tom Whitney remarked, adroitly changing the subject. Meredith had to hand it to him: he had social diplomacy down to a fine art. 'I don't believe I'm familiar with the label. May I?'

'It's my own blend,' Henry said, presenting the bottle with pride. 'If you like, after dinner I'll take you down and show you my wine-room. I have nearly two hundred bottles laid by, and another ten gallons ready to be racked in a couple of weeks.'

'Remarkable,' Tom murmured, and bathed the ladies in a winning smile. 'I can't remember when I last enjoyed a meal so much.'

'Exactly what was it that brought you here?' Bill suddenly asked. Of all of them, he was the only one not completely captivated by Tom Whitney's presence.

Meredith, who'd been secretly relishing the fact, almost dropped her fork on Lucille's precious china plate at the question, and sought frantically in her mind for a plausible explanation. On the other hand, reasons dictated that in a few hours they were all going to find out what he had in store for them, so why should she try to spare him their distress? 'He came to——'

'To see Meredith,' Tom finished, looking her straight in the eye.

So she was Meredith now, was she? 'Among other things,' she continued. 'But Mr Whitney also has plans for this house, and I think it's time you all heard about them.'

Eleanor, painfully shy at the best of times, astounded Meredith then by reaching over and patting their landlord lovingly on the arm. 'This is his house,' she said in her timid little voice. 'He's come home again, haven't you, Tommy?'

Just for a moment, an expression that was close to vulnerable crossed Tom Whitney's face, but it was gone so quickly that Meredith wondered if she'd imagined it. 'Not exactly, Mrs Kennedy,' he said gently. 'It's been a long time since this was home to me.'

'What plans?' Bill persisted.

'Far-reaching,' Dolores suddenly piped up. 'I read the leaves this afternoon, and they showed changes.'

Lucille, who didn't hold with what she termed 'gypsy nonsense', snorted elegantly. 'No doubt they told you a tall dark stranger was going to cross our threshold, Dolores.'

'Well, if they did, they were right, weren't they?' Dolores' black eyes snapped with pleasure. She liked nothing better than to engage Lucille in verbal battle.

Meredith could see they were in danger of getting side-tracked again. 'Why don't you tell us what you plan to do with this house, Mr Whitney?'

'Why don't you stop being so formal, and call me Tom like everyone else?' he countered pleasantly, and smiled at her.

His gaze softened when he smiled, she noticed, caused in part by long, straight lashes that swept down to shade the brilliant blue eyes. It was a very attractive smile—a very attractive face, really. Strong, clean lines that came from good bone-structure, and the kind of thick, dark hair that had to be kept cut short to prevent it from running wild. He was the sort of man who would age very grace-fully. While other men grew bald and amiable, he'd turn silver and suave.

He was also a man unused to losing, she reminded herself. A man without conscience when it came to a fight. If he'd been surly and bellig-erent, she'd have known what she was up against and could have challenged him head-on. But he was far too clever to employ such direct tactics. He knew precisely what he was doing when he favoured her with that smile.

He was probably a lawyer, she thought. Andrew had always maintained that, in order to succeed in the legal profession, a man had to be both devious and heartless. 'They're all a bunch of crooks,' he'd declared once.

Yet Meredith couldn't quite shake the memory of the look she'd caught on her landlord's face a moment ago, when all his ingrained sophistication had fallen apart long enough to reveal a glimpse of a much younger, much less assured Tom Whitney. Eleanor's innocent remark to him had uncovered a deep and secret hurt of some kind, but he'd covered it up and, instead of lashing out at the old lady, he'd answered her with a kindness and respect that Meredith couldn't fault. She almost wished he hadn't. She didn't need his redeeming qualities to surface now. Acknowledging them could weaken her cause.

'What do you do for a living?' she asked him abruptly.

He raised his brows in an expression that almost made her blush with shame. No need to sound so bitchy, it said. 'I'm a lawyer,' he told her mildly.

'How interesting,' Lucille gushed. 'What is your area of expertise, Thomas?'

'I specialise in matrimonial law, Mrs Delong.'

Meredith couldn't contain the flash of malice that sprang up inside her. She ought to have known he'd be the kind of man who'd get rich on other people's personal misfortunes.

*   *   *

Tom saw the glint in her eye and suppressed a sigh. For a little while, he'd thought he was making headway with her. At one point she'd almost smiled at him, and the tension that had sharpened all her delicious curves into angles had eased its grip. In repose, her expression became sweetly reflective, and he'd found himself unable to look away from her. Did she know that, when she forgot to be abrasive, her eyes grew softly luminous and took on the colour of deep, still pools touched by moonlight? Or that the curve of her cheek was as tender as a child's?

It was an image that did not last nearly long enough. Her question and his answer seemed to heighten her misgivings. The glare she flung his way reminded him that she was a woman fiercely dedicated to the people whose interests she'd undertaken to protect, and that she found him beneath contempt.

He envied her her absolute certainty, and wished his own assurance weren't becoming so riddled with doubt. After he'd read the newspaper article, he'd come to the house knowing exactly what he expected to find: some avaricious woman, with a thickening middle and a hard face, fleecing a bunch of helpless retirees of their livelihood.

He'd felt doubly justified in terminating the lease then, convinced he was doing the old folks a favour. He'd told himself they'd be better served in a proper home, a place where there were ramps for wheelchairs, and bathtubs with grab bars. A place where the doorways were wide enough for hospital beds to roll through, and uniformed attendants were on duty around the clock. But that had been before, when he'd envisaged the people he was evicting as faceless and enfeebled strangers.

He'd broken one of the first rules of litigation by assuming that the other party could spring no surprises on him because he had prepared for every eventuality. Quite simply, he'd underestimated the opposition. A more vital, energetic group of elders was hard to imagine, and if tonight's meal was any example there wasn't a jury in the land that would convict Meredith of avarice. On the contrary, she was almost certainly subsidising the household expenses from her own cash reserves. As for hard-faced—hell, her expression when she looked at her 'family' would move the stoniest judge to tears.

Tom sighed inwardly. She moved *him*, for Pete's sake, and he liked to think he was a tough nut to crack. She made him want to give in to her, to make things easier for her, no matter what it might cost him.

But damn it all, this was his house to do with as he pleased, and up until a couple of hours ago it had pleased him to sell the property. He'd come back to Riverbridge to sever his last ties with a time and a place he preferred to forget, not to get embroiled in the problems of a bunch of people who weren't his responsibility. Meredith's name was the one on the lease; *she* was his tenant, and if she'd chosen to sublet without his consent or knowledge then she must bear the consequences of such action. Legally, he was absolutely within his rights to carry through with his original plan. The only problem was, legalities didn't seem to be worth much when they were measured against the happiness and well-being of individuals like these folks.

'I have a rather fine port downstairs,' Henry said, breaking the uncomfortable silence that had fallen over the table. 'Perhaps you'd like to sample it, son, while I show you my wine-room?'

'Perhaps,' Meredith said in that aggressive tone of hers, 'he'd also like to take a look at the mildew stains on the walls where the damp seeps through the foundations in winter.'

'Or the attic ceiling,' Bill threw in. 'Every time it rains, we find a new leak.'

Yesterday's Thomas Whitney would have said: what do you expect for the sort of rent you pay, the Ritz? Now he heard himself ask sharply, 'Why didn't anyone tell me?'

'Meredith went up on the roof to see what she could do about the leak,' Prudence informed him. 'My heart was in my mouth the whole time, I can tell you.'

Horrified, he swung his gaze to Meredith. 'Don't ever do that again, do you hear me? That's a job for an expert, and even they wouldn't tackle that slope when the roof is wet.'

Her eyes shot sparks. 'We couldn't afford an expert, and our landlord didn't seem to be interested.'

'In order to be interested, Meredith,' he chided her, 'he had to be informed.'

The air crackled with tension. Sensing it, Henry pushed back his chair. 'It's not raining now,' he complained, 'and I'd have thought my port would take precedence over a few damp spots. Humour an old man, Tom, and let me show off my wine-room to you.'

Tom was glad of the excuse to leave the table. Meredith's eyes accused him, no matter how much he tried to ignore them. And no matter how hard he tried, he couldn't shake the guilt she inspired in him.

'What a lovely young man,' Prudence sighed the moment he left the room with Henry. 'And so good-looking!'

Bill clicked his tongue impatiently. 'Looks are only skin-deep, Prudence, as a woman your age ought to know by now.'

'But his smile is kind.' Unperturbed, Prudence started to clear the table. 'I've lived long enough to know that you can tell a lot about a person by the way he smiles.'

'And you can't condemn a man because of his face,' Florence chipped in. 'He can't help the way he looks, after all.'

'It's what's behind the looks that bothers me,' Bill muttered.

'What's disturbing you, William,' Lucille declared loftily, 'is that he's an educated and worldly gentleman whose interests extend beyond aphids and the latest pesticides for roses.'

'You're what disturbs me,' Bill retorted, 'because you're not nearly as smart as you'd like to think you are. In fact, Lucille, sometimes you're downright silly.'

Ignoring Lucille's gasp of outrage, he pressed a hand to his chest in disgust, and Dolores, who was loading a tray with dirty glasses, shook with laughter. 'What's the matter, Bill? Did something you eat disagree with you?'

'Having Tom Whitney around is enough to give anyone indigestion,' he grumbled.

Prudence tilted her head to one side consideringly. 'Aren't you being a bit hard on him? I think he's very charming.'

'He is,' Bill agreed. 'That's what worries me. He's not the type to put himself out unless he's after something.'

Eleanor, who was so quiet most of the time that people tended to forget she was in the room, surprised them all by speaking out for the second time that evening. 'He's a nice boy,' she said. 'Now that he's come home again, he'll take care of us, won't he, Meredith? He'll fix the roof, and he won't let people look in the windows and frighten us any more.'

'That's not why he's here,' Meredith said hastily, her amusement at the general response to Tom Whitney's sudden appearance on their doorstep evaporating at Eleanor's words.

If there was one person who truly needed someone to stand between her and the real world, it was Eleanor. She was a refugee from a bygone era, a refined, soft-hearted creature who believed that all men were chivalrous defenders of women and virtue. Whatever hardships she'd endured, she'd remained as trusting as a child, totally incapable of suspecting a person's motives. 'He hasn't come to help us at all, Eleanor,' Meredith said gently.

'When are you going to tell us what he does want?' Bill demanded. 'You keep hinting about something, Meredith, and I think it's high time you stopped beating around the bush and told us what it is. We're not children, you know. Whatever it is, we'll deal with it.'

With the possible exception of Eleanor, he was right on every count, Meredith realised. It was unfair of her to keep them guessing about something which affected all their lives so deeply. She drew in a deep, reluctant breath. 'He's evicting us,' she told them. 'We've got two months to find another place.'

For a moment, no one uttered a sound, then Prudence let out a thin wail of distress. 'Don't let him do that, Meredith,' she begged. 'Don't let him make us go into one of those old folks' homes. People only go there to die.'

'Why would he do such a thing?' Equally distraught, Florence let the plates she was collecting clatter down on the table, and Meredith realised the full extent of everyone's shock when Lucille let the incident pass without comment.

'We pay the rent on time,' Florence went on, wringing her hands. 'We keep the place up as well as we're able. Why won't he let us stay here?'

'Because he doesn't care,' Bill said bitterly. 'You haven't lived here long enough to remember him when he was a boy, but I have. He never cared, not about anyone. It wouldn't have mattered to him if the whole town had fallen in the river and drowned. He wouldn't have lost any sleep over it.'

Dolores reached into her pocket for the pills she always carried with her. Noticing her pallor, Meredith pulled out a chair. 'Sit down, Dolores. Are you having chest pains again?'

'They'll pass, they always do . . . as long as I take my pills.' Dolores never complained, but her lips were compressed with pain and her breathing was shallow.

'You must try not to worry,' Meredith urged. 'You'll make yourself ill if you do, and I'm going to need all of you to help me work out a solution to this problem.'

Eleanor stroked Dolores' hair fondly and, although none of the others touched her, their eyes were full of concern and affection, even Lucille's.

Dolores' mouth relaxed into the beginning of a smile, and she reached up to squeeze Eleanor's hand. 'There,' she said, in a more normal tone. 'I'm all over it now, so you can stop looking so tragic. It's going to take more than an eviction notice to kill me.'

'By God,' Bill fumed, his strongly marked brows drawn together with anger, 'if I were twenty years younger I'd take that young upstart outside and give him the thrashing he deserves.'

Just then, the sound of footsteps on the cellar stairs alerted them to the fact that Henry and their dinner guest had finished touring the wine-room.

'Perhaps we shouldn't let him know that...' Meredith began, then stopped. It was too late. Even before she could have finished the sentence, Tom Whitney was in the doorway, and all it took was one look around for him to realise that something was terribly amiss.

'Why is everyone looking so upset?' he asked, sounding for all the world as if he really cared. 'Did something happen while we were downstairs?'

CHAPTER THREE

'I TOLD them,' Meredith said.

Tom's blue eyes were full of reproach. 'I wish you hadn't done that, Meredith.'

'I'm sure you do. It would have been much easier for you if I'd waited until after you'd gone, wouldn't it?'

'It would have been much easier on everyone if you'd given us time to work out a compromise.'

Eleanor clasped her hands and gave a happy little sigh. 'Oh, I knew he'd look after us in the end! Didn't I tell you so, Meredith?'

'What sort of compromise?' Bill wanted to know, his jaw thrust out belligerently. 'A rent increase, maybe?'

Prudence had started crying as soon as Henry walked into the room. He put his arms around her and rocked her gently, a puzzled expression on his face. 'What on earth is everyone talking about?'

'He's kicking us out of the house,' Bill said shortly, jerking his head to indicate Tom.

Henry's aristocratic features flushed with indignation. 'Good lord, what a waste of vintage port!' he exclaimed.

'Look,' Tom began, 'can't we discuss this without everyone getting in an uproar?'

'What is there to say, if you've made up your mind?' Henry asked severely. 'Quite frankly, young man, I think our time would be better employed looking for another house, and furthermore, we have every right to get in an uproar, as you choose to call it.'

Florence went to stand in front of Tom, her fists planted on her hips. 'Don't you even care about what happens to us? Doesn't it bother you at all to know we could end up in some retirement home where they push mashed-up food in a person's face, without any regard for whether or not the stuff's fit to eat in the first place?'

'I think you're over-reacting, Mrs Widdowes. I'm sure the homes you're talking about aren't really all that bad.'

'They're worse, some of them,' Bill snapped, 'but don't let that keep you awake at nights. We're not your problem, Tom Whitney, and that's one thing at least that we can be grateful for.'

'Henry,' Prudence sobbed, 'if we have to go into a home, they'll put us in separate parts of the building, and we'll only see each other at meal-times and when they make us all play bingo.'

'I hate bingo,' Dolores said mournfully.

'Bingo is for the feeble-minded,' Lucille decreed, 'and I would absolutely refuse to participate in such a pastime.'

'Hush, precious,' Henry murmured consolingly to Prudence. 'We won't be separated, I promise you. Somehow, we'll find a way to stay together, you'll see.'

Meredith watched despair sap all the joy out of the faces of the people she loved so much, and wished she'd found another way to break the news to them. She wished, too, that Tom Whitney would

fix his gaze some place else than at her. She didn't
care for the expression in his eyes.

'I'm going to make us some tea,' she said, then
added as an afterthought, 'Except for you, Mr
Whitney. You can do us all a favour and leave.' She
flung him a disgusted glare and stalked off to the
kitchen.

Undeterred, he followed her. 'I hope you're satisfied,' he said. 'If you wanted to paint me as the
villain of the piece, you've certainly succeeded.'

'And you fit the role amazingly well,' she
retorted, running water into the kettle.

'Look, Meredith, how was I supposed to know
you'd filled the house with old people?'

'What difference would it have made if you had?'

'Damn!' All at once, anger spilled over, pinching
the corners of his mouth and turning his eyes a pale
and steely blue. 'I do believe you'd be disappointed
if I were to tell you I've changed my mind.'

'Have you?'

'I'm prepared to take the matter under consideration,' he hedged.

She almost sneered at him. 'Spoken just like a
lawyer!'

'What's that supposed to mean?'

'I've heard all about you, Thomas Whitney,' she
snapped, setting the kettle on the stove with a bang.
'I know how you feel about this town and the
people who live in it, and your sudden concern for
the residents of this house is too little and too late.'

He lunged towards her suddenly, and before she
had time to move away he had her trapped between
him and the kitchen cabinet. Planting his hands on
either side of her, he leaned on the counter-top, his

arms almost brushing hers. 'You don't know the first thing about me,' he said with soft menace, 'and I don't feel the need to explain myself to someone who thrives on ancient gossip.'

He was standing very close. Meredith leaned as far back as she could, but he simply curved over her so that she had no choice but to stare up at him. She could see how long and fine his lashes were, could detect the hint of port on his breath, the lingering trace of aftershave on his skin. His teeth were very even, very white, and his mouth was not smiling.

'Are you telling me the rumours aren't true?' To her annoyance, her voice trembled a little as though she was nervous, or unsure. He was very good at putting people on the defensive, she thought.

'Would you believe me if I did?'

She hated his habit of answering a question with a question. It made her feel that he was always one step ahead of her, setting traps and waiting for her to convict herself out of her own mouth. 'I might. It would depend . . .'

'Depend on what, Meredith?'

She swallowed and looked him full in the eye. At her back, the drawer-handle poked wickedly into her spine. 'On what you had to say, of course.'

'I would tell you the truth, if that's what you're wondering.'

'Even if you did,' she said, 'it wouldn't help us find another place to live. Don't you see that that's what really matters?'

The kettle began to whimper, little puffs of sound that died away then repeated themselves a bit more forcefully. Some of the steel in Tom's gaze had softened, and his brows were knit in thought. 'Will you agree to a truce until I have time to think a few things through?' he asked. 'I'm really not completely without feeling, regardless of what you might have heard.'

She wanted very much to believe him. It might be crazy, but she found herself remembering that moment at dinner when he'd looked like a little boy trying very hard not to let anyone see that he cared what people thought of him. How foolish! He was the most self-contained man she'd ever met. Even the flash of anger she'd aroused in him had been brought under immediate control.

And yet . . . She ventured a glance up at him, and saw things she hadn't wanted to admit to before. Gentleness and strength in his expression—and more. The line of his jaw bespoke determination, but there was passion in the curve of his lips, and something about the way he was watching her, his gaze utterly candid and deliberate, that made her heart falter.

What would it have been like to meet him in different circumstances? she wondered. Would there have been this antagonism? This mistrust? Or would they have smiled at each other, the way a man and a woman did when something new and exciting flickered into life between them? Might he not then have taken this private moment alone with her to bend his head so that his lips could brush hers with a message that said, I like you, and I want you to like me?

He was so still that he might have been listening to her thoughts. She wrenched them back to the question he'd asked her. 'Yes,' she breathed, 'I'll agree to a truce.'

His eyes, which had been so intently staring into hers, dropped to her mouth and examined it with scrupulous care. 'Thank you,' he said, and there was such intimacy in his voice that he might as well have kissed her. The seconds ticked by, delicate as spun glass.

Impatient at being ignored, the kettle emitted a shrill burst of sound, and the moment was shattered. 'Make the tea, Meredith,' Tom ordered softly, 'and I'll let myself out, but I'll be in touch within a day or so.'

He called her on Tuesday morning. 'Have lunch with me,' he said. 'I think I've come up with a solution.'

All the time that she was getting dressed, she kept telling herself that it was just a business lunch. She was meeting him at the hotel, which probably meant they'd eat in the hotel dining-room in full view of all the regulars and anyone else who felt disposed to lunch on pan-fried sole and peas. There was no reason at all for her to be flinging one outfit after another on to her bed, as though what she wore would in any way affect the outcome of their meeting.

In the end, she chose a white pleated skirt and a cotton knit top of glacier-pale green because it was, quite simply, the coolest, most comfortable outfit for such a hot day. The only reason she added a thin gold chain around her neck was that her good luck charm hung on it, and she figured she needed all the luck she could command. As for the cologne and the mascara, they were just to bolster her courage. A woman always felt more confident if she knew she looked her best.

He was sitting in one of the lobby's plum-coloured velvet armchairs when she arrived, with his right ankle propped on his left knee. He wasn't wearing either a tie or a jacket, and from his post behind the front desk Darby Bradford was directing black looks his way, as though Tom were guilty of public indecency.

Not that Tom seemed intimidated, Meredith noticed. He was glowering right back. 'Sorry I'm late,' she said, approaching him.

He stood up and his dark expression lessened somewhat. 'You're not,' he replied, taking her elbow and steering her across the lobby, 'but, even if you were, you'd have been worth the wait. You look lovely.'

'Thank you.' Uneasily, she withdrew her arm, conscious of Darby shifting along behind the desk so that he could enjoy an unimpaired view of what was going on. His brows lowered over his disapproving old eyes, indicating plainly enough what he thought of Andrew Blake's widow's allowing herself to be seen in such company.

Their arrival in the dining-room provoked a similar response. Conversation lapsed as heads turned to follow their progress across the thick carpet to a table by the window.

Tom waited until they'd placed their order, then leaned back in his chair and examined her, his clear blue gaze taking note of her face, her hair, her clothes, in a manner that was almost clinically impersonal. 'Before we get down to business,' he said, 'will you tell me why a woman your age is content to waste her youth acting as nursemaid to a bunch of people old enough to be her parents?'

'They're my family,' she started to explain. 'I told you the other day——'

'I know what you told me the other day, Meredith. What I'm asking you now is why you're making do with them instead of going after the real thing. Why aren't you looking for a husband who can give you children to nurture?'

'I had a husband and——'

'I know about that, too. Andrew Blake, the semi-invalid war veteran. He taught chemistry at the high school when I was a student there, and he must have been pushing forty then. How old was he when you married him, Meredith?'

'Forty-four, so your calculations are off.'

'But not by all that much. What was he—fifteen, twenty years older than you?'

Her response was instantly defensive. 'What does his age matter, or his health? He was a wonderful man. Ask anyone in town, they'll tell you the same thing. He gave me more happiness in the two years we were together than I'd ever known before.'

Tom raised sceptical brows. 'But he's been dead almost four years, so why aren't you getting on with your life? Or are you telling me you won't sully his memory by taking another man in your bed?'

What an insensitive clod he was! she thought, spots of anger blooming on her cheeks. No wonder the glances directed his way by the other patrons were full of such unvarnished disfavour.

And yet, hidden deep under her anger, was the uncomfortable knowledge that Tom Whitney had come close to exposing a truth she'd never really confronted before. They had shared a different kind of marriage, she and Andrew, a more intellectual union than most, based on contentment and spiritual fulfilment. He had needed her in a way that no one else ever had, and for the first time she had really *mattered* to someone. She had looked after him and made him happy, and one of the reasons she'd chosen to stay in his home town was the solace she had derived from being his widow.

He had died tragically after a fire in his lab at the school had endangered the lives of four students. Thanks to him they'd escaped unharmed, but the smoke inhalation had been more than Andrew's one good lung could handle, and suddenly Meredith had found herself alone again. Except that this time was different. The affection and respect that had been afforded to him during his lifetime had been transferred to her after his death. She was Mrs Andrew Blake, young widow of a man whose bravery both at home and abroad was legend. Not only had this made the early days of her grief more bearable but, for the first time ever, Meredith had felt part of the continuity that marked other people's lives and which had always been conspicuously lacking in her own. She wasn't just a figure passing through. She had a past. She belonged.

She'd never doubted that she had loved Andrew, nor ever questioned the reasons for doing so—until now, when she suddenly found herself wondering if it had been *because* he'd needed her so badly. Was that why she sometimes woke up in the night, yearning for something...someone?...not passively, as she had with Andrew, but with a hunger that embarrassed her when she remembered it in the dispassionate light of day? Was that why her imagination had been set on fire the other night in the kitchen, with Tom Whitney looming over her, blotting out her awareness of everything but the surging intimacy of his gaze?

Those same blue eyes penetrated her thoughts now, piercing the memories and recalling the question that had prompted such unsettling introspection. 'The reason I've not remarried,' she told him, 'is that the right man hasn't come along, that's all.'

'He's never likely to, at this rate. You have to get back in the mainstream for that to happen.'

'Go shopping for a husband, you mean? Advertise my availability?' She curled her lip in distaste. 'No, thank you.'

Tom buttered a roll and nodded approval of the wine which the waiter displayed for him. 'Just pour it,' he said dismissively, and turned his attention back on Meredith. 'In my line of work, I've come across a lot of women who do exactly that. They almost make a career out of parasitic relationships.'

Parasitic? Her relationship with Andrew had *not* been parasitic, and what it had been was none of Tom Whitney's business. 'I'm not like a lot of women.'

'Yes, you are, Meredith,' he scoffed with stinging disdain. 'You're afraid of taking chances, afraid of life. You want to be safe, so what do you do? First you marry someone old enough to be your father, then you latch on to a collection of elderly cats who are so damn grateful for your attention that they don't even stop to ask themselves why you bother.

Both are just variations of the clichéd "old man—child bride" theme. You don't really want a husband, you want a father—and, in the present case, a mother, too.'

He struck with such a cruel and devastating perception that her eyes filled with tears. 'And what if I do?' she muttered, fumbling in her bag for a tissue and unable to find one. 'What's wrong with that, as long as I'm not hurting anyone else?'

'Use your napkin,' he said, a trace of regret warming his voice, 'and for heaven's sake don't start crying. I'm not trying to upset you. I'm just curious, that's all.'

She dabbed at her eyes with the starched linen. 'You're an unfeeling wretch. I bet you never once questioned what it would have been like to grow up without parents who loved you.'

'That's where you're wrong,' he said in a strangely flat voice, and she caught a glimpse of something stark in his eyes that vanished as quickly as it arose. 'My parents didn't love me, they tolerated me.'

'Oh, rubbish! You were probably an impossible child.'

'I'm sure I was. Unhappy children often are impossible.'

Meredith couldn't see what he'd had to be unhappy about. He'd known who his parents were, hadn't he? Known a place he could call home? 'Why were you so miserable?'

He shrugged. 'I was an unplanned mid-life baby. What might have been interpreted by some as a miracle struck my parents more as an indictment for having succumbed to carnal desire. Theirs,' he said with undisguised bitterness, 'was a punitive and unforgiving God. Enjoyment or pleasure were deemed sinful, temptations laid out by the devil, and I grew up in an atmosphere so devoid of joy or love that my childhood memories are almost entirely without warmth of any kind.'

He stared out of the window at the shining river flowing quietly past the bottom of the hotel garden. His eyes, Meredith noticed, were a bleak and brilliant blue—and as lacking in warmth as his memories. 'But you must have had some happy times, surely? You were their son. Maybe they were too reserved to let you see it, but they must have loved you.'

'How charmingly naïve of you, Meredith!' His laughter was neither kind nor amused. 'Do you know what my mother used to tell me? That she didn't set foot outside the house once the evidence of her pregnancy became apparent. She was a God-fearing woman, she said, and would not flaunt her shame in public.'

'But that was Victorian!'

'It was unforgivable. I cut my teeth on the knowledge that I was nothing but a cross my parents had to bear. Unfortunately for them, I wasn't a submissive child. I rebelled every chance I got, took delight in defying them, got myself into more scrapes than I can remember, and, through it all, they suffered—visibly and publicly.'

He paused to drain his glass and seemed to find the wine bitter on his tongue. 'There wasn't a soul in town who didn't know what a burden had been thrust upon their weary shoulders,' he finished. 'I ran away for the first time when I was six, and kept on doing it until I was seventeen, when they finally stopped being dutiful and, to our mutual relief, let me go.'

'Was there nothing good you remember?' She was stunned by the image he had conjured up, of a lonely, unhappy little boy whose only way to gain attention had been to misbehave. Even she, displaced foster-child though she'd so often felt herself to be, had never been treated with deliberate cruelty.

'My father's younger sister, Nellie,' he said almost dreamily. 'She was my godmother as well as my aunt, and she lived with us until I was about three or four. I remember she had soft hands and a soft voice and she used to sing to me sometimes.'

'What happened to her? Did she die?'

He stared down at his empty glass. 'She might as well have. She married a poet and went to live in California, against my father's wishes. He disowned her and I wasn't allowed to mention her name again, but I missed her for the longest time.'

He splashed more wine into his glass, his expression remote, and Meredith sensed he was uncomfortable at sharing so much of himself with a stranger. 'At least you knew who you were and where you belonged,' she said. 'I grew up in foster homes and used to be afraid to go to sleep in case I died and no one would even notice I wasn't there any more. I wanted to be part of a family more than anything else in the world.'

'So you borrowed other people's, which brings me back to my original question. When are you going to go after what you really want, Meredith, instead of settling for half-measures?' His eyes swept over her again, boldly appraising. 'You're still young, you're not bad-looking, you're reasonably intelligent. There's no reason you can't find another husband.'

Still young? Not *bad*-looking? *Reasonably* intelligent? Meredith rested her fork on the side of her plate, afraid she'd choke if she tried to swallow. She'd never entertained thoughts that she was beautiful or anything, but the way he enumerated her assets left her feeling plain beyond redemption, and, although she couldn't imagine why it should matter, the idea that he found her so unremarkable hurt. 'Are you offering yourself as a candidate?' she enquired, with a brave attempt at humour.

His grimace was an outright insult. 'Hell, no!' he exclaimed, then added belatedly, as though it occurred to him that his reply had been something less than flattering, 'In my job, I see too many disasters to have much faith in the durability of marriage. I'm not interested——'

She had heard quite enough. 'I was joking, for heaven's sake! I'm not interested, either.' Especially not in a man like you! 'What does interest me is the solution you've come up with for the house. Can we get down to specifics and try to settle things? I'd like to be able to reassure the rest of the family when I get home.'

'Very well.' He reached over and topped up her glass, then his own. 'Ideally, I'd like to sell the property to you outright, but I take it that's not really an option?'

She shook her head. 'Unfortunately not.'

'I thought I'd mention it anyway.' He shrugged. 'You're a widow, after all, and there might have been some money.'

'There was very little,' Meredith replied levelly. 'Not every wife comes out of marriage a rich woman, whatever you might like to think.'

'OK, OK!' He sighed and held up his hands in a gesture of surrender. 'Then I'll give you an extension on the lease for as long as you need it, on the understanding that you make every effort to find other accommodation as soon as possible, and in any event within one year, after which time the house goes on the market regardless. If I can find a buyer who's interested in continuing your lease, I will, but my primary aim is to get rid of the place. First of all, I want to put the money to another use; second, it's costing me more in property taxes than I'm collecting in rent, and last...' he drew in his breath and cast a disparaging glance around the dining-room '...I don't want any reason ever to have to come back here again.'

It wasn't perfect, but then, she knew better than most that things seldom were. At least it was better than what he'd offered before, and she had a year to search out an acceptable alternative.

'Well?' He was watching her closely again. 'Do we have a deal?'

'We have a deal.' She took the hand he extended across the table and shook it. 'Thank you.'

'I'll draw up an informal agreement whereby you're free to vacate without notice if you find another place, and I'll drop it off at the house before I head back east tomorrow.'

'You're leaving so soon?' She couldn't imagine why, but something vaguely resembling disappointment surged through her at the news.

He smiled at her, and she thought what a truly attractive man he was when he wasn't scowling or being insulting. 'I can't think of any reason for me to stay, can you?'

'No, of course not.' What on earth was wrong with her? He wasn't the only attractive man in town, and in any case she wasn't looking for involvement. But the disappointment persisted.

'Would you care for dessert? Coffee?'

'Nothing, thanks. I should be getting back.' She gathered up her bag and pushed back her chair, anxious suddenly to be away from him. 'Thank you again for lunch—and for everything else.'

'I'll walk you out to the street.' He was beside her, his hand again at her elbow, his head inclined towards hers as he continued, 'Think about what I said, Meredith. Sooner or later, you're going to find yourself alone again, you know. The old folks can't live forever, and you might be better off using the coming year to settle them some place where they'll be comfortable and well cared for, so that you'll be free to live your own life.'

Around them, the other diners watched, their eyes cold and judgemental, and for the first time their covert interference jarred on Meredith. It was as if their condemnation of Tom reached out to touch her, too, and she found herself resenting it. What business was it of theirs whom she chose to have lunch with? And why should she share their disapproval of him?

'I'll think about it,' she said, knowing she was unlikely to change her mind.

He pushed at the revolving door, ushering her through and following her into the street. The sun was almost directly overhead and fiercely hot, but there was a haze around it that spelled a change in weather. 'We're going to have a storm,' he predicted, squinting up at the sky. 'Maybe it'll clear the air a bit.' He grinned at her engagingly. 'Maybe it'll rid the atmosphere of the pollution created by that dreadful Tom Whitney's showing up in town again.'

He stood on the pavement, a tall, powerfully built, utterly self-assured man, but all at once the little boy looked out of his eyes again, and even all these years later he was still hurting. Unexpectedly, Meredith wanted to put her arms around him and hug him. Instead, she mumbled goodbye and turned away, telling herself they'd both have been shocked if she'd given in to the impulse.

He hadn't had a good night. The storm had broken shortly after midnight and not worn itself out until just before dawn. He would have liked to be able to say that that was what had kept him awake, but the truth of the matter was, he was worried. About her. About her coping with leaking roofs and damp cellars and all the other myriad things that could go wrong with a house that was almost a hundred years old.

When was the last time the furnace had been serviced? Or the chimneys swept? Who shovelled snow from the steps in winter so that the old folks didn't slip and break a leg?

He thought of her small, soft hands all calloused from doing chores that rightly belonged to a man, and muttered under his breath. He didn't want to care. She'd invited problems, choosing to live in the house and taking on the supervision of the old people. She wasn't a child, even if she was no bigger than a fourteen-year-old, and she wasn't his responsibility.

But he kept seeing her eyes, twice the size they should have been in that small face, and as clear as creek-water running over polished grey stones. They advertised a quality of innocence—of un-awakening—which, if she'd been his wife, would have been replaced long ago by knowledge.

Furious at the direction of his thoughts, he swung around the curve in the driveway and came to an abrupt halt at the sight of all the old folks milling about under the big copper beech that shaded the west side of the house. Against the trunk, the men were endeavouring to hold a ladder steady on the rain-slippery grass. The women were darting about them like agitated little birds, and they were all, without exception, gazing up into the branches of the tree. Even from a distance, Tom knew imme-diately that something was wrong.

CHAPTER FOUR

THE problem, Tom shortly discovered, was the family's other cat, a young male tabby called Albert. Spooked by the thunder of the previous night, he'd climbed up in the beech tree and, if the old ladies were to be believed, apparently couldn't make his way down again. What concerned Tom, however, was the fact that Meredith was at the top of a ladder that should have been consigned to the rubbish dump at least ten years ago, and was hanging dangerously far off to one side, trying to coax the animal into her arms.

'Come down from there at once, Meredith!' Tom roared, his breath constricting in his chest as the foot of the ladder slithered precariously on the grass. Covering ground like a long-distance runner, he elbowed Henry and Bill aside and grasped hold of the rungs to anchor it.

Meredith's disembodied voice floated down to him. 'Don't shout, you'll frighten him off again— oh, drat! Now see what you've gone and done!'

'What's happened?'

'Is Albert safe?'

'Be careful, dear...' The voices rose in anxious chorus.

'He's jumped up on the attic gable.' Meredith's ankle appeared above Tom's head, followed shortly thereafter by her legs clad in blue denim cut-offs. 'I'll have to go up on the roof to get him now.'

'This is all your fault,' Bill advised Tom testily. 'We were doing all right 'til you showed up and started trying to tell us how to go about our business.'

'I noticed,' Tom replied with heavy sarcasm. Reaching up to help Meredith down the last few rungs, he couldn't quite resist giving her a little shake as she touched solid ground. 'I thought I told you to stay off ladders.'

'Stop fussing,' she replied breathlessly. 'Albert's up on the roof and I've got to get him down before he panics and falls.'

'He won't fall, and even if he does he'll survive. Cats always land on their feet.'

She flung him an incredulous stare. 'From three floors up? Don't be ridiculous!'

'You're not going up on that roof, Meredith.'

'Really? Who's going to stop me?'

'I am.' Tom heaved an exasperated sigh. He knew he should have dropped the agreement in the post and headed out of town first thing this morning, instead of giving in to his urge to see her one more time. 'If anyone has to rescue the damned cat, I will.'

'He won't let you near him. You're a stranger.'

'You said the same thing about his mate.'

'Let him do it, Meredith,' Henry urged. 'He's right, you know. It isn't a job for a woman.'

'I agree.' Bill couldn't keep the satisfaction out of his voice. 'If anyone's going to break a neck, better it's his than yours.'

Eleanor's soft brown eyes grew round with apprehension. 'Oh, Tommy, be careful,' she begged.

Her concern touched him. 'Don't worry, Mrs Kennedy. It won't be the first time I've climbed around up there.'

'The easiest way is to go out through one of the attic windows,' Meredith said, taking three steps to keep pace with each one of his as he started towards the house. 'If you really insist on doing this, that is.'

'I know.' Brusquely, he shrugged aside her advice. It was obvious enough that, with the exception of Eleanor, none of them cared a bit if he fell to his death. 'I used to live here, remember?'

'I'm just trying to help.'

'I can manage.' They were inside the house by then, making their way up the main staircase. Tom knew he sounded ungracious, but he couldn't help himself. Looking around at all the closed doors to the bedrooms gave him the strangest sense of *déjà vu*. He'd always been shut out of things in this house.

Memories, unpleasant for the most part, crept out of the corners and slid over him as he climbed the much narrower stairs to the attic. It was still full of junk, trunks and furniture draped in musty old bedspreads and dust-cloths. He'd been terrified of this part of the house when he was a kid, ever since the time his father had shut him up here as punishment for one of his many misdemeanours. That was what had originally driven him to explore the roof. Hiding out between the chimney-pots and gables had given him a false sense of freedom.

'You won't be able to get that open,' Meredith informed him as he tugged at the window that looked out into the branches of the copper beech.

'The only one that works is over here. All the rest
are stuck.'

The attic was like an oven. Heat crouched under
the sloping angles of the roof, while at shoulder-
level sunlight struggled through the dusty south-east
windows to reveal water-stains running down the
brick facings of the chimneystacks. Scattered
around the floor were pails and dishpans of various
sizes, some of them more than half full of rain
water. The guilt which Meredith so easily inspired
in Tom rose up anew at the sight. 'Once the cat's
safe,' he said, in an effort to assuage his conscience, 'I'll oil all the window-hinges so that you
can air out this whole room.'

Pushing open the window she'd indicated, he
eased himself out on to the wide, gabled sill and
stood up. He could see clear up the sloping roof to
where a scrawny little cat huddled against the base
of one of the chimneys. The sun hadn't reached
this side of the house yet, and the shingles were still
slick from last night's rain.

'Well, here goes,' he muttered, bracing himself
against the side of the gable and hauling himself
up until he was astride its peak. At least he was
wearing topsiders with non-slip soles. How disappointed Bill must be if he'd noticed.

'Maybe if I were to try calling Albert,' Meredith
suggested, leaning out of the window from the waist
up to watch, 'he might come down and meet you
halfway.'

'Just as long as that's all you try to do.' Deciding
he needed all his concentration for the task at hand,
Tom pushed away the thought of Meredith clam-
bering around out here trying to fix leaks, and

scrambled up the slope towards the ridge of the roof, his fingers searching out hidden holds and his toes digging into the crevices between the shingles. In this instance, at least, his memories had deceived him; scaling the roof wasn't nearly as easy as it had seemed when he was a boy. In fact, it was downright dangerous, and for the first time he knew a glimmer of sympathy for his mother. Maybe his escapades had been responsible for her grey hairs, after all.

Once he was within grabbing distance of the cat, he reached out one hand and, feeling like a fool, tried imitating Meredith's soft coos of encouragement. 'Here, Albert, be a good kitty and come to Tom.'

The cat eyed him malevolently, waited until he almost had a grip on it, then backed around the chimney. Straddling the ridge, Tom inched his way forward until he could stand upright against the stack.

Up this close, it was easy to see why there were water-stains running down the masonry facings inside the attic. The flashing had come away from the brick in half a dozen places. As for the roof itself, it needed to be replaced entirely. The shingles were paper-thin, curled up at the ends and split from years of winter frosts and frying summer heat. No wonder the whole thing leaked every time it rained.

Deceived by his stillness, the cat ventured around the base of the chimney to sniff at his ankles. Hanging on to the brickwork with one hand, Tom bent and swept him up by the scruff of the neck, ignoring the outraged hiss that accompanied the capture. 'Come here, you little menace, before you get us both killed.'

He wished again that he'd stayed away this morning; that he'd never come back to town in the first place; or, failing both these options, that he could turn his back on the whole mess now and simply walk away. Instead, he was as helpless as the cat he held clutched in one hand; caught in a situation that grew increasingly complex with every passing minute and, to his enormous disgust, incapable of ignoring it.

Once Tom disappeared out of sight, Meredith had to rely on her ears to tell her how he was progressing, and the lengthy silence left her taut with apprehension. Not that he struck her as physically inept. He had the build of an athlete, and she'd noticed the co-ordination of his movements, his free and easy stride, and the way he'd swung himself out on to the sill in one smooth, effortless move.

Yet her uneasiness lingered, and she was honest enough to admit that it stemmed from something more than concern for his safety. He gave the impression of coiled energy, of a mind seldom at rest, and it would be a mistake to let his impressive physique blind her to other facets of his personality. There was no ignoring the sharp intelligence in those blue eyes, or the determination that moulded his jaw. He would, she thought, make a very good friend—or a very bad enemy.

What was taking him so long? Leaning out, she craned her neck in an attempt to spot his progress. 'Tom? Are you all right?'

'Yeah.' She heard his grunt of annoyance. 'At least I will be when I unload this cat. Keep clear of the window—I'm on my way back.'

She knew from experience that coming down the roof was easier than climbing up. There were enough valleys between the gables and various other architectural projections to offer safe landing spots even for a man his size, and it was apparent from the steady sound he made that he was well in control of his descent.

He swung himself across the sill with Albert clinging to his shoulder. 'Don't try to unpeel him yet!' he snapped, when she reached out to take the frightened cat from him. 'Just move back and let me inside before we have to go through the whole operation again.'

Not until the window was closed would he allow her to unhook the claws that had driven through the fabric of his shirt and implanted themselves in his skin. 'Poor baby,' Meredith murmured, freeing one paw after the other with gentle fingers until she could lift Albert clear. 'When are you going to learn not to climb trees?'

'I hope he's had all his shots,' Tom muttered sourly, unbuttoning his shirt and slipping it off his arm so that he could inspect the row of tiny puncture wounds in his shoulder.

Meredith, who was nuzzling the cat, looked up indignantly. 'Of course he has! I wouldn't neglect an animal any more than I would a human being.'

For some reason, her reply seemed to amuse him. He treated her to one of his charming grins. 'In that case, how about a little sympathy for me? I'm bleeding, see?'

She saw that his shoulder was evenly tanned and firmly muscled and broad enough to accommodate a woman's head with ease. And at the same instant, she became aware of the silence surrounding them and of their isolation from everyone else in the house.

His words were as plaintive as a little boy's and, if that was all he'd been, she'd have dabbed at the bright specks with the tail of his shirt and offered to kiss them better. But the smooth expanse of flesh belonged to a man who made her uncomfortably aware that she was a woman. She didn't want to look at him; even less did she want to have to touch him, not because she didn't trust him but because she wasn't sure she could trust herself.

'Come down to the kitchen if you're worried,' she said briskly, skirting the pails and pans to lead the way downstairs, 'and we'll get Dolores to treat your injuries. She's a much better nurse than I.'

The family had congregated on the back veranda. Florence had brought out a pitcher of fresh lemonade and a plate of home-made sugar cookies. Meredith deposited Albert on the floor next to his food bowl and left Siamantha to sniff him over and wash his ears. 'Mr Whitney needs some antiseptic for his shoulder, Dolores,' she said, and wondered why Tom looked so disgruntled. Everyone was being properly grateful for his rescue mission. Prudence and Henry made room for him beside them on the swing, and Lucille, wearing a large straw hat trimmed with silk roses, seated herself opposite and poured lemonade for him with regal grace. Eleanor hovered over him like a faded butterfly too restless to settle in one spot, but her gaze was so clearly full of affection that he couldn't possible mistake her intention. Even Bill's face had assumed a slightly less hostile expression.

'We're so thankful, Tom,' Florence began, offering him a cookie.

'Oh, my goodness, yes!' Prudence agreed. 'We really hate it when Meredith has to go up on the roof, but you see, Mr Whitney, none of the rest of us is quite able.'

'And that particular cat,' Lucille observed, 'is rather a fool, Thomas. He's forever falling over something.' She sniffed. 'He shows a marked lack of breeding, I fear.'

'Strays often do,' Dolores remarked slyly, with a meaningful look in Lucille's direction. 'Let me see where you got scratched, Tom.'

Henry cleared his throat. 'While we're on the subject of gratitude, there's one other thing we'd like to mention. As you must be aware, we're extremely fond of this old house, my boy. The thought of having to leave it was distressing, and we were very relieved to hear from Meredith that you've changed your mind about evicting us.'

'Actually,' Tom said, wincing as Dolores dabbed at his scratches with iodine, 'I've been giving this business of the house some extra thought, and——'

'Oh, we understand we'll have to move eventually,' Henry rushed on nervously, 'but at least now we have a bit more time to find somewhere else.'

'That's not what's bothering me.' Tom drew in a breath as though, Meredith thought, watching the expressions flit over his face, he'd found himself unwillingly backed into a corner. 'I'm concerned at the number of things needing attention. Windows that don't open or close properly, loose shingles, that sort of thing.'

'We do our best,' Bill said defensively. 'This house is a lot like us—wearing out. What else can you expect, considering its age?'

'Which is why,' Tom continued, steadily ignoring the interruption, 'I thought I'd spend part of my vacation fixing a few things up so that you're at least able to keep dry and warm through the winter.'

'Oh, Tommy!' Eleanor's face grew radiant with joy. 'You're going to stay, after all.'

'Just for a little while, Mrs Kennedy.'

'I knew you were a decent man,' Dolores said complacently. 'The leaves are seldom wrong.'

'We could write out a list of things that need fixing,' Bill went so far as to offer, 'and we'd be glad to lend a hand where we can.'

'But not until after lunch,' Florence said. 'If he's going to help us out a bit, the least we can do is feed the man, so let's start by fixing some sandwiches. Bill, will you bring in a few radishes and some fresh lettuce from the garden while Henry slices up the ham?'

'I shall prepare my special mustard,' Lucille announced, in her *grande dame* fashion. 'Eleanor, make yourself useful and cut some sweet peas for the table, and if you're very careful I'll allow you to arrange them in my crystal vase.'

They bustled about, collecting empty glasses and chattering animatedly among themselves, thrilled at the promise of a little excitement in their lives.

Meredith waited until she and Tom were alone before she spoke. She was well aware that, of all of them, she'd been conspicuously silent in her expression of gratitude. The truth was that, once again, he'd touched her deeply. It was a habit that she found very disconcerting, but that didn't make his offer any less generous. 'Thank you,' she said, as soon as they had the veranda to themselves. 'This is really nice of you.'

'I'd be more inclined to value your opinion,' he retorted with some bitterness, 'if you didn't sound so amazed.'

She shrugged. 'I admit I'm surprised. I thought you couldn't wait to get out of here. What changed your mind?'

He looked at her, his bright blue gaze intent, and for a moment she felt that odd electricity hum between them again. She wondered how she'd respond if he were to reply, You did. He stirred things in her that she couldn't turn away from, yet at the same time she sensed that he was dangerous and that if she didn't stay on guard against him he could destroy the life she'd built for herself and leave her with nothing but broken pieces that wouldn't fit together again.

'Well, I didn't make the offer to win points with you,' he said, destroying any illusions she might have harboured before they had time to take root.

His tone was so cutting that she felt herself flush with the sting of it. 'Then why are you being so generous?'

Idly, he buttoned up his shirt and strolled over to where she was perched on the veranda railing. 'I can spare the time, and it will be cheaper than calling in professional help. The place should probably be condemned, and I see no point in sending good money after bad.'

Well, that certainly told her where his priorities lay. 'I don't want to inconvenience you.'

He laughed outright at that, but there was no real warmth in the sound. 'Hell, Meredith, you've been inconveniencing me ever since the day I set foot in town. Don't stop now.'

'Why are you so angry?' she asked curiously. 'You weren't pressured into volunteering your services.'

Abruptly, he reached out and tilted her chin so that she was staring up into his eyes. 'I was pressured,' he retorted softly, his words fanning over her mouth in warm little eddies. 'I know it, and so do you. And I'm angry because I'd rather walk away, and instead I'm staying here because the thought of you climbing around on that rotting ladder makes me break out in a cold sweat.' His gaze grew hard. 'But don't take advantage, Meredith. I'm not really the domestic type.'

His voice was barely above a whisper, but she knew he intended the words as a threat. 'You're pinching my chin,' she said, jerking herself free of his fingers. 'And if the fact that the ladder's falling apart is causing you so much grief, why don't you just offer to buy us a new one and let it go at that?'

'If I were half as smart as I like to think I am,' he said, stepping away from her, 'I'd do precisely as you suggest. But some latent grain of decency tells me that it won't hurt me to put myself out for a few days. Call it my good deed for the year, if you like.'

'In that case,' she said, 'let's get down to business without delay. The sooner we begin, the sooner we'll be done, and the sooner you'll be free to leave with a clear conscience.'

'My sentiments exactly,' he said. She almost shivered at his tone.

Of course, things didn't work out quite that simply. The problem with old houses, Meredith soon discovered, was that one repair invariably led to another. And then there was another complication which she hadn't foreseen. For all that they were anxious to do whatever they could to help, the rest of the family didn't have too much time or energy to spare after they'd looked after all their other responsibilities and interests—which left Meredith to fill the role of Tom's assistant.

He was not easy to please. 'I suppose I'll have to rent a truck,' he said gloomily, the day he and Meredith went down to the building supply yard to order materials. 'That two-bit car of yours can't handle this sort of thing.'

Meredith was rather fond of her 1978 Chevrolet. It was old, but it had served her well. 'It wasn't meant to haul lumber,' she retorted.

'It's barely able to haul you,' he said disparagingly. 'Is the truck rental outfit still next to the *Times* office?'

'Yes.' Her answer was barely out before he was striding off down the road, and she found herself practically running to keep up with him. 'Look, I know you're in a hurry to be finished, but do you think you could slow down just a little bit? My legs aren't like yours.'

As had occasionally happened before, her reply seemed to amuse him and dissipate his ill-humour. 'I noticed, and it's a fact which helps make my protracted stay here slightly more bearable,' he drawled, his scowl melting and his gaze roaming lazily over her face. 'Why, Meredith, am I making you blush?'

'No,' she snapped. 'You're making me suspicious. I'm not used to you being pleasant.'

They had reached the rental office. She was halfway through the door he held open for her when he looped a finger around one of her curls and tugged her gently to a stop. 'If you were a city woman,' he said, grinning down at her so infectiously that she found herself smiling back, 'I think I might enjoy making you suspicious more often.'

From behind the front desk, Cal Gibson, the proprietor, looked up and slammed closed his order book. 'You got business here, Tom Whitney, or were you just passing through?' he demanded, the antagonism in his tone splintering the moment.

Tom straightened and brushed by Meredith. 'I want to rent a vehicle.'

'Pity. I ain't got any cars to spare. Reckon you'll have to leave town on foot, same as you did the first time.'

'I'm looking for a truck.'

'Ain't got any of them, either.'

'There are four around the back. I noticed them on my way over.'

'They're taken.'

'I don't think so, Mr Gibson.' Tom spread his feet apart and planted his fists on his hips, as though he intended to remain there for the rest of time if that was what was necessary for him to get served.

'Well, la-di-da! Mr Gibson now, is it?' Cal sneered. 'You learn some fancy manners back east in the big city, Tom Whitney, or are you just pretending, so you can impress all us small town folks with how *sophisticated* you are?'

Meredith couldn't believe what she was hearing. She knew Cal. He played the banjo at the annual town picnic and grew prize-winning dahlias that left Bill green with envy. He was a nice man, with a wife, two grown sons, and a golden retriever, all of whom he adored. She'd have sworn he was incapable of such rudeness if she hadn't witnessed it at first-hand.

Tom reached into the back pocket of his blue jeans, pulled out his wallet, and slapped his driver's licence and his American Express card on the counter. 'I believe refusing service to a qualified customer is a breach of contract that could cost you your franchise, Mr Gibson,' he remarked evenly. 'Now, do I get a truck? Or do I make a phone call at your expense and lay a complaint against you?'

There was a silence that lasted several seconds during which Tom and Cal Gibson glared at each other. Cal was the first to drop his gaze. 'Fill in the form,' he muttered, more surly than ever, and shoved an application across the counter before turning to a row of keys hanging on brass hooks on the wall behind him. 'You got any special preference, *Mr* Whitney?'

'The half-ton.'

The keys shot across the counter and crashed against Tom's wrist. Meredith saw his lips tighten in anger, but he said nothing. His application complete, he waited for Cal to return his licence and credit card, then turned to the door. 'Let's go, Meredith,' he ordered, weighing the keys lightly in the palm of his hand.

As usual, he was out on the pavement before he'd finished speaking. Cal's voice halted Meredith as she prepared to follow. 'How come you're keeping company with the likes of him, Meredith? Tom Whitney's not your type.'

'He's doing some work on the house, Cal, that's all.'

'And what's it going to cost you, girl?'

'Nothing. He's just looking after his property.'

Cal's voice lowered ominously. 'He's not the sort to do something for nothing, Meredith. You'll pay, one way or another, mark my words. I just hope you don't find the price too high, that's all.'

'Meredith!' Tom reappeard in the doorway, bristling with impatience.

'Reckon you'd better run along,' Cal advised her. 'Wouldn't do to keep the big man waiting, now would it?'

'Good grief!' she exclaimed, once she and Tom were in the truck. 'What did you ever do to Cal to make him behave like that?'

'Like what?'

Meredith's mouth fell open. 'He was insulting, Tom! You must have noticed.'

Tom shrugged. 'He was as usual,' he said indifferently. 'I'd have been more inclined to take notice if he'd been cordial. I told you before, Meredith, I'm not exactly Riverbridge's favourite son.'

That was true; he had told her before and there'd been a time when she'd accepted everyone's poor opinion of him. She'd even shared it as recently as a week ago. Five days ago, to be more accurate. Yet now she found herself wanting to defend him. He'd probably deserved his reputation before. Perhaps he *had* been a thoughtless, irresponsible rogue when he was younger, but he'd obviously changed. A rogue wouldn't have agreed to extend her lease, or forfeited his summer vacation to fix up a house so that other people could live there more comfortably. A rogue definitely would not have rescued Albert.

'They're being unfair to you,' she said fiercely, 'and I've a good mind to tell them so.'

He turned to her at that, a mocking light in his eyes, and at first she thought he was going to laugh at her. But his expression sobered, and to her surprise he slid his arm across the back of the truck seat and drew her close. 'Save your breath,' he murmured against her mouth. And then he kissed her, probably not for very long and probably not very wickedly. His lips closed on hers quite gently, then shifted as though they were searching for something. And then they settled, as if they'd found what they'd been looking for.

Meredith saw his eyes widen briefly, as though *he* was surprised as well, and then her own fell shut because the sun was suddenly too dazzling and so were the feelings racing through her. She slipped her hand up alongside his jaw, wanting to hold him close, wanting to prolong the wonder he'd aroused in her.

Unfortunately, he did not seem similarly inclined. He lifted his head and put her from him firmly, although when he spoke, his voice sounded cracked and rather hoarse. 'That was the first of two mistakes,' he said.

'What was the second?' she asked, trying to mask her disappointment.

'We got caught. The vigilantes were watching.'

Following the direction of his narrowed glance, she saw Cal Gibson and Joshua Hartley standing on the pavement. She didn't need to hear what they were saying. It was plain enough from the expressions on their faces that they had indeed witnessed the kiss, and that they considered her guilty of committing the most unforgivable indiscretion.

CHAPTER FIVE

IN THE days that followed, a number of small changes occurred which, taken separately, amounted to little. Overall, however, they began to make a difference. Most noticeably, the property's rather dilapidated air slowly disappeared, chased away as much by the activity taking place as by any major repair. Tom's energy was unflagging, and Meredith couldn't quite decide if it was dedication to his self-appointed task that drove him, or just his desire to have it over and done with so that he could leave with a clear conscience.

From early morning until daylight faded around nine at night he measured and sawed, hammered and nailed, and lost his temper. 'Nothing is square!' he raged, at least six times a day, and on those occasions Meredith learned to fade quietly into the background until he'd wrestled his frustrations under control. Sometimes his language made her blush.

July and August were always hot, but this year temperatures exceeded all previous records. The first few days on the job, Tom wore blue jeans and a short-sleeved cotton shirt. By mid-morning, he was stripped to the waist and Meredith, who was often assigned to holding one end of the measuring tape, spent a lot of time studying him while he assessed the house.

She had to keep reminding herself that, intellectually, she scorned women who focused exclusively on a man's physical assets, and she tried to relegate her preoccupation with Tom to a purely aesthetic appreciation for a well-conditioned body operating at peak performance. Admiring the complex rhythm of Tom's muscles under skin which grew ever more deeply tanned was not much different, she reasoned, from enjoying watching a gymnast demonstrate his skills.

When he showed up one morning wearing khaki shorts, she indulged in a little impersonal reverence for the elegant strength of his legs, telling herself she expected nothing less from a man who'd confessed to a fondness for skiing, swimming and windsurfing. These were not, after all, sports for the physically under-endowed.

But when he'd suddenly glance up from a task and smile at her for no good reason, his teeth dazzling and his eyes brilliant in his dark face, she had a much harder time rationalising her feelings. The heat that raced through her then was no more intellectual than the melting warmth she experienced when she saw his big, strong hands lift Eleanor clean off her feet and deposit her gently on the veranda to save her climbing over a pile of lumber.

Even stranger was the pleasure that Meredith derived from earning his praise for a job well done. She basked in his approval, and pushed away the thought that her reaction was out of all proportion to her accomplishment.

'I should hire you full time and start a business,' he teased her once. 'We make a great team.'

She hoarded statements like that, the way other people saved money for a rainy day, and refused to ask herself why. Nor did she dare question her preposterous urge to defend him when he was maligned around town, even though anyone less in need of her intercession was hard to envisage. All she knew was that her loyalty, once so firmly entrenched on the side of the locals, was slowly shifting over to the opposition, a fact which became embarrassingly clear the day she undertook to run several small errands for Tom.

'Good morning, Len,' she said, breezing into the building supply yard and scanning her shopping list. 'I need a pound of one-and-a-half-inch galvanised finishing nails, a tube of silicone sealant, four sheets of coarse sandpaper, four sheets of medium—oh, and some glue.'

Stonily, Len Mackie, who owned the building supply yard, started stacking the items on the counter. 'What sort of glue?'

Struck by his unsociable tone, Meredith glanced up. 'Well, it's for a number of different things, Len, so I suppose I should take that multi-purpose white stuff. It doesn't make sense to buy six different types if one will do, wouldn't you say?'

'I'd say it doesn't make sense for Andrew Blake's widow to be carrying on with someone like Tom Whitney,' Len informed her sourly. 'You've always been so level-headed, and now look at you. Tom Whitney doesn't belong in this town, and you shouldn't be encouraging him to stay.'

'As far as I'm concerned, he's welcome to stay as long as he pleases,' Meredith said stiffly. 'I don't care what the town thinks. He's been a tremendous help to us, and that's what matters. For the first time since we've lived there, the house is going to be weatherproof this winter.'

'I swear I don't understand you, Meredith. Nobody does. You're defiling Andrew's memory, having that man under your roof.'

'It's his roof, too.' She swept up the bag of supplies, and abandoned any attempt at further pleasantries. 'Put this on our account, please. Good day.'

At least most of the family were solidly behind Tom. 'I don't know why you want to waste money on a hotel-room when you could sleep here,' Florence told him more than once.

'You don't have enough room, for a start,' Tom replied, the first time the subject arose.

'Eleanor and I could double up and let you have one of our rooms,' Dolores had offered, but he'd refused to put them to so much trouble. Meredith had been secretly relieved. Having him under the roof both night and day would invite even more local censure. Also, she needed a little time away from him to regroup her thoughts which, when he was around, tended to become fixed on matters irrelevant to the normal tempo of things. She couldn't afford to forget that he was only a temporary fixture in her life.

For different reasons, Bill also had reservations about Tom. 'He's doing a good job, I'll grant you that,' he'd admit, when the others praised the repairs and renovations, but he'd always qualify the compliment with, 'but I'll be just as glad when he's done and gone. A leopard doesn't change his spots, and he'll show himself for what he really is, sooner or later. I don't want him causing trouble in this house.'

Meredith noticed Bill's gaze rested moodily on her at such times, as though he saw more than he was prepared to discuss. He was the only member of the family who'd lived in Riverbridge when Tom was a boy, and Meredith suspected that he was privy to more local gossip than the rest of them.

She wondered if he'd heard about the day Tom had rented the truck; the day of the kiss. Of all the memories she was hoarding, this one glowed the brightest, probably, she acknowledged, because it stood in such isolated splendour. To her unwilling regret, Tom had not shown any inclination to repeat the incident. In fact, he seemed anxious to keep physical contact with her to a minimum, though she knew by then that no one in town would believe her if she said so.

'If you'll paint this trim now,' he'd say, 'I can get on with repairing the cracked plaster over there.'

There was always a two-by-four, or a can of paint, or a ladder, between them. Until the night of the barbecue, when everything changed.

That afternoon, a squabble erupted in the kitchen. Meredith never was able to ascertain whether it was the weather or the lamb that caused the trouble. The heat was hard on the old people, and they tended to become short-tempered with each other. All Meredith knew was that when Florence and Dolores came back from one of their trips to the farmers' market with a whole loin of lamb for dinner Lucille gave vent to an outburst of annoyance that soon involved everyone but Tom, who was outside fixing a drainpipe, and Meredith, who was sweeping up debris from repairs to the door leading from the kitchen to the back porch.

'I suppose your famous tea leaves told you to make our lives miserable by sticking a roast in the oven on a day when it's ninety degrees inside and any normal person would settle for something civilised like cold salmon,' Lucille spat at Dolores.

'If I were to follow through on everything I read in the leaves,' Meredith heard Dolores retort, 'I'd stick you in the oven.'

'Well, really!' Lucille's indignation echoed through the entire house. 'How dare you speak to me in such a manner, you common little gypsy?'

'Call me names, and I'll put a hex on you,' Dolores promised.

Bill flung down his pipe. 'Women!' he muttered, and stamped past Meredith to find peace in his garden.

'Don't fight,' Prudence begged. 'It's not ladylike.'

'And it's hot enough in here without you two getting all riled up,' Florence put in.

Lucille quelled them with a glare. 'Don't interfere! I will not be spoken to like that.'

'Don't raise your voice at Prudence,' Henry warned her. 'I won't stand for it.'

'One would think,' Lucille declared, 'that Prudence were a child, the way you rush to her defence all the time.'

'You're all behaving like children,' Florence announced. 'Get out of my kitchen and fight somewhere else, or you won't be eating anything tonight.'

Meredith dropped the broom, ready to act as referee, but Tom got there ahead of her. 'How about a barbecue, folks?' he enquired, poking his head through the open window.

'We don't own an outdoor grill,' Henry told him.

'I'll build one for you. All it takes is a few bricks and one of the oven shelves for a rack. Have a picnic in the back garden for a change. It'll be a lot cooler out there.'

Eleanor, who hated discord, inched her way back into the kitchen. 'Will you stay and eat with us, Tommy?' she whispered.

He leaned further in the window, and eyed the loin of lamb. 'I might, if you twist my arm. That meat looks pretty good to me. Meredith, take the truck into town and pick up a sack of charcoal, and while you're down there, maybe you'd stop by the lumber yard and buy another gallon of paint for the window trim, and a roll of weatherstripping for the doors.'

'And some ice-cream, Meredith,' Florence added, rummaging around in the freezer and coming up empty-handed. 'Bill brought in raspberries from the garden, but I don't have anything to serve with them.'

'I'd offer to make shortcake,' Dolores said, 'but I wouldn't want to upset her ladyship by turning on the oven.'

Lucille, who had a very sweet tooth, struggled briefly with her pride, then conceded, 'I could live with a little extra heat for the length of time it takes to bake shortcake.'

When Meredith returned from town, everyone was on speaking terms again. Tom had the barbecue pit ready, and Henry had helped him set up a makeshift table with two sawhorses and a sheet of plywood. Prudence and Eleanor were busy bringing out dishes and an old sheet for a table-cloth, and Bill was shucking corn freshly picked from the vegetable patch.

By the time the sun had slipped behind the cottonwoods, the air was fragrant with hickory smoke and roasting lamb, and harmony reigned again. Henry poured home-made cider for everyone, and Meredith, sitting propped against a tree-trunk with Tom sprawled at her feet, looked around and thought that she could learn to become very content with such a life.

Henry raised his glass in Tom's direction. 'The house is beginning to shape up, my boy.'

'It must have been a showpiece in its earlier days,' Dolores said, as the murmurs of agreement subsided.

'It was,' Bill put in unexpectedly. He seldom talked about the past. All any of them knew was that he'd been a widower for a good many years and that there'd never been another woman for him after his wife died. 'Even forty years ago, when there were fine old homes all along this side of the street, this was the best. Always neat as a pin, never any peeling paint or broken windows. Mind you, labour was a lot cheaper in those days.' He sighed. 'It's a pity things have to change.'

'I remember it as always being dark,' Tom said, staring up at the first sprinkling of stars. 'And very quiet, as though someone had just died. I don't think I ever heard anyone laugh here, except when I was very young.'

'I have something to show you, Tommy,' Eleanor confided, apparently reminded of something by his comments. 'A little surprise, just for you.' She drifted off across the lawn to the back door and disappeared inside the house.

Lucille shook her head. 'What has she found now, I wonder? She collects things, you know,' she told Tom. 'I've seen her poking around in the attic, looking through those old boxes and trunks. I suppose she can't help herself. She has so few things herself. When Meredith first found her, she was carrying everything she owned in two plastic shopping-bags.'

Florence looked up from basting the lamb. 'I didn't know that's how——' she started to say, when they all heard the sound. A thready scream of pure terror, it seemed to hang in the quiet evening air.

For a split second, no one moved, then pandemonium broke out. 'That was Eleanor!' Henry exclaimed, struggling to his feet and almost tripping over the cats. Prudence clung to his arm, her face even paler than usual.

'She's in trouble,' Dolores began, knocking over her lawn chair in her haste. But before they'd properly gathered their wits Tom was sprinting towards the house with Meredith not far behind him. She raced through the back door and into the hall in time to see him scoop Eleanor up from where she had collapsed just outside her bedroom door, and seat her in the wing-chair that stood near the post table.

'She's shaking like a leaf,' he said, 'but I don't think she's actually hurt.'

'Eleanor.' Meredith took one of the old lady's hands and chafed it gently between her own. 'Eleanor, try to tell us what happened.'

Eleanor clutched at Meredith. 'He was here
again,' she said faintly, her eyes wide and staring
towards where the front door stood open to let in
a breath of air. 'He came right in the house.
Meredith, I'm so frightened of him.'

'What's she talking about?' Tom muttered.
'Who's "he"?'

Meredith cast a quick glance over her shoulder.
'I wish we could keep this from the rest of the
family,' she whispered. 'It just gets everyone upset.'

'Well, you can't,' Tom told her impatiently.
'They're all coming through the kitchen now.
What's going on here, Meredith?'

'Someone might have been peering in the
windows at night.'

'What do you mean, "might have been"? Have
you called the police?'

Meredith looked uneasy. 'No.'

'Why ever not? That's what they're there for.'

The rest of the family arrived on the scene again.
'What's happened?' Bill panted, leading the pack.
'Eleanor, have you hurt yourself?'

'Are you ill? Do you have a pain?' Prudence
asked, slipping an arm around her shoulders. 'My
goodness, Eleanor, you're so cold, and you're
shivering. Henry, get her a shawl or something.'

'Shock,' Dolores decided, touching Eleanor's
brow with a practised hand. 'You're all clammy,
love. What brought this on?'

'I saw him again,' Eleanor whispered, then
cringed when Lucille clicked her teeth in exasperation. 'I did, Lucille. He was right inside the house
this time.'

'What does he look like, love?' Florence asked, draping the shawl Henry had brought around Eleanor's frail shoulders. 'Can you describe him to us?'

'Did he say anything?' Bill demanded.

'Is he someone we know?' Prudence asked.

Eleanor's eyes filled with tears. 'I don't know,' she whimpered. 'I can't tell you.'

'Of course she can't,' Lucille said. 'It amazes me how she's able to see things the rest of us miss, but she can *never* describe what it is she claims to have seen.'

'Be quiet!' Tom snapped, apparently unaware that no one adopted that sort of tone with Lucille. 'And stop trying to intimidate her.' Kneeling in front of Eleanor, he took both her hands in his. 'Mrs Kennedy...Eleanor,' he said gently, 'do you know who this person is?'

'I don't know,' she repeated, her eyes darting about as if she feared the intruder would pop out of the woodwork.

'Did he speak to you, Eleanor?'

She nodded. 'Yes, Tommy.'

'What did he say?'

'He said...' Her eyes filled with tears. 'He said...that if I told anyone...' Then her voice broke, and she dropped her head forward until it rested on Tom's shoulder.

He reached up one hand and stroked her soft grey hair. 'Did he threaten you, Eleanor?'

She nodded, and swallowed a sob.

Henry and Bill, who'd gone out to inspect the front garden, came back at that moment. 'There's no one out there now,' Henry said. 'Don't be afraid,

Eleanor. You chased him away. He won't be back again tonight.'

She raised her head at that. 'But he might, later—when I'm by myself again.'

'How often have you seen him?' Tom enquired.

She lifted her shoulders. 'Maybe three or four times,' she said doubtfully.

'Has anyone else seen him?'

'No, Tommy. He only talks to me, because he knows I'm afraid.'

Lucille drew in an irate breath, as though she were about to voice another unsympathetic opinion, then she caught Tom's gaze fixed on her and changed her mind.

'Eleanor's bedroom's on the ground floor,' Henry murmured. 'I rather think that might be why she's the only one who sees this person.'

'That could change if he's now taken to coming inside the house,' Tom observed. 'You do make sure the doors are locked every night, don't you, Meredith?'

'Of course.'

He nodded, his brows knitted in thought. 'Is it possible he's looking for a place to stay? That he's——?'

'What? Another one like us, you mean?' Bill flared. 'I don't recall having to resort to frightening anyone by sneaking about when I arrived. I walked up and knocked on the front door, with all my wits where they belonged and my manners in place.'

'I'm not trying to be offensive,' Tom started to say, then noticed Eleanor shaking her head in denial. 'What is it, Eleanor?'

'He's not like us,' she said, clasping her hands nervously. 'He isn't old and poor.'

'That settles it, then.' Tom stood up. 'He might be harmless, whoever he is, but to be on the safe side I think we should notify the police and have them keep an eye on the place. It can't hurt.'

Henry picked up the phone. 'Shall we call them now?'

'No.' Tom shook his head. 'If it's all the same to you, I'll stop by the station in the morning and file an official request. What I think we should do now is go back to our barbecue, but before we do...' he strode down the hall to the front door '...we'll close and lock this. No point in making things easy for him, whoever he is.'

The lamb, laced with garlic and rosemary, was delectable, the corn succulent, the potatoes crisp on the outside and tender on the inside. Dolores' shortcake melted on the tongue, and the raspberries fairly burst with juice and flavour, but the spontaneity of the evening had been killed. It would take more than good food and home-made cider to resurrect it, Meredith realised, looking around.

They were all trying, but the simple truth was that they were perturbed, each of them for different reasons, perhaps, but perturbed none the less. It showed in the expression on Bill's face, a mixture of outrage and frustration that his eighty-two years prevented him from assuming the role of protective male in a predominantly female household.

It was evident in the way Henry and Prudence sat close beside each other and held hands, and in Lucille's erect posture which was meant to convey her disdain for a lot of nonsense even though her eyes darted nervously about the garden, looking for the intruder she professed didn't really exist.

It showed in the way Florence and Dolores closed ranks around Eleanor, who sat silent as a wraith and couldn't swallow a morsel of her tiny portion of food. Even the cats were touched by it. Siamantha voiced her uneasiness in near-flawless Siamese fashion, while Albert prowled restively under the table, seeking human comfort wherever he could find it.

Tom spoke, his voice relieving the brooding tension. 'If that invitation to stay overnight is still open,' he said, 'I wouldn't mind taking you up on it, just this once. I could sleep on the couch in the TV-room.'

It was an inspired suggestion. The TV-room was next to Eleanor's bedroom and, even though the prowler was unlikely to show up twice in one night, just knowing Tom was nearby went a long way towards restoring her confidence. 'We'll all be safe with you here, Tommy,' she said, the ghost of a smile lighting up her face.

'I don't see how all of you is going to fit on that couch,' Florence said, eyeing him doubtfully. 'It's about eighteen inches too short.'

He grinned. 'That's OK, Florence. It won't be the first time I've slept with my feet hanging off the end of the bed. If I'm too uncomfortable, I can always camp out on the floor.'

Lucille hid a ladylike yawn behind one hand. 'I think I shall retire for the night,' she decided, rising and nodding graciously to the rest of them. 'One way and another, it has been an exhausting day.'

'Not until you've helped with the dishes, you won't,' Dolores told her. 'We're not leaving this mess until morning.'

'We'll all help,' Meredith said, anxious to avoid any more confrontations.

But Dolores wouldn't hear of it. 'No, Meredith. If you must do something, make up a bed on the couch for Tom. After the day you've both put in, it makes sense that *you'd* be tired,' she said, with a pointed glance at Lucille, 'and if the seven of us can't manage a little thing like dishes by ourselves, then perhaps we do belong in a retirement home, after all.'

It was a suggestion that suffused Lucille with fresh energy. Meredith, on her way to the TV-room with an armful of bed linen, noticed Tom following behind and trying to hide a grin.

'Dolores could give me lessons on handling Lucille,' he said admiringly. 'I guess I was pretty short with the old dear earlier.'

'Don't feel bad. Sometimes, that's the best way to deal with Lucille,' Meredith replied, spreading a sheet over the couch, 'and you were very sweet to Eleanor, which is what really matters.'

'You're sounding surprised again, Meredith,' he chided her, stuffing a pillow into a slip. 'What did you expect? That I'd laugh at her?'

'No, of course not. I wonder what it was she wanted to show you.'

'Lucille was probably right about that. I dare say Eleanor found something in the attic that belonged to my family, and she thought I'd be interested in seeing it.'

'And you wouldn't be?' The bed made up, Meredith switched off the lamp to keep out the moths flitting around outside, then went to stand at the open window.

Tom clicked the door closed, shutting out the light spilling in from the hall, and joined her. 'No.'

'Couldn't you pretend to be, if it means that much to her?'

'I'm not very good at pretending, Meredith.'

'I think a little pretence can sometimes help us get over the rough spots,' Meredith murmured.

'But you can't run away from reality. It isn't smart. I mean, here we are, fixing up a house that we both know...' He hesitated, then went on a little savagely, 'You don't do anyone any favours by ignoring the inevitable.'

She turned towards him. He was just another shadow in the room, a little darker than the rest except for the faint pearly light reflecting off his shirt. 'Is that what you think I'm doing?' she asked softly. 'Just because I want to make every day count for people who might not have too many left to enjoy?'

'Stop trying to touch me, Meredith,' he warned.

Her eyes flew wide in the gloom. 'I'm not touching you,' she protested.

His hand shot out and snared her wrist. 'Yes, you are,' he contradicted, pulling her against him. 'You're touching me in places I don't want to know about.' His mouth brushed over hers briefly. 'That I don't want *you* to know about.'

He sounded almost angry, she thought, and for the space of a heartbeat he held her away from him. Then his mouth swept over hers a second time, possessively, desperately, and he was begging for things she'd never had to give before, his hands seeking, and the rest of him—all that beautiful body that she'd tried so hard to dismiss as irrelevant—urgent and alive against hers.

Meredith was sharply conscious of the scents surrounding them. Of honeysuckle and roses and summertime drifting through the open window; of cider and the sweet tartness of raspberries on his lips. In that moment, she knew that what she'd yearned to discover in the solitude of her lonely bed was suddenly very close, and she wanted to experience it, very badly.

Unashamed, she relaxed against the male strength of him and let her fingertips encounter the texture of the sun-darkened flesh she'd admired from a distance. She felt his heart lurch, heard his breath snag, and then his lips were at her throat, searching out the triangular hollow of her collarbone, inching inside the loosened top of her blouse and down towards her breast.

She ached with an intensity that hinged on pain; heard the blood rushing through her veins; felt the world, fragrant with another scent that she recognised as passion, slip sideways.

Then, shockingly, it was all over. He put her from him so roughly, she staggered. 'This is what I meant when I talked about pretence,' he said unsteadily. 'This isn't real, Meredith, and it's no use our pretending that it is.'

He swung out of the room, cursing when he barked his shins on the end of the couch, and left her with the harsh echo of his breathing for company. She felt as if she'd been dealt a killing blow, and knew she'd never again taste raspberries without remembering this stolen moment, this midsummer night that was neither a dream nor reality. And she, who thought she'd known loss and loneliness in their bleakest forms, had never before felt so impoverished in her life.

CHAPTER SIX

BY NINE the next morning, when Tom paid a visit to the police station, the heat was sweltering enough to sour more than the old folks' tempers.

'You claim that a person or persons unknown have been trespassing on the Whitney property, that same person or persons have been upsetting one of the residents,' Abel Myers, Chief of Police, repeated, laconically scribbling notes. 'Funny something like this should start happening right after you show up back in town. Do you mind telling me where you were last night, and why this is any of your business?'

Tom was in no mood to take abuse from Abel Myers, whom he would have supposed, had he spared him any thought at all in recent years, to have retired long ago. 'It's my business, Chief Myers,' he said shortly to the man who'd been a persistent thorn in his side throughout his youth, 'because I'm making it my business. Some person or persons are trespassing on *my* property and upsetting the residents of *my* house. I came to register one complaint, but if you keep on harassing me this way I'll make that two.'

'No need to get short with me, boy. It's my job to ask questions. Rumour has it you're passing yourself off as a big-city lawyer these days, so you ought to know that without me having to spell it out for you.' Chief Myers' mean little eyes squinted out of the pink expanse of his face, making him look, Tom thought uncharitably, more like a pig than ever. 'Now, exactly where were you yesterday evening when the purported incident took place?'

Tom held his temper in check with difficulty. 'At the house as a dinner guest. There are eight witnesses who can testify to that.'

'And where'd you go after that?'

'I——' On the verge of telling the truth, Tom stopped. To admit he'd spent the night at the house would stir up nothing but trouble, and from his perspective he already had more of that than he could handle.

To know that he'd held Meredith in his arms, that he'd given in to the craving that had tormented him for days, was tough enough. That he also had to live with the memory of how close he'd come to letting her innocence and generosity goad him into taking everything she'd been so willing to offer was something he'd prefer to forget. No one else would ever know how the taste of her, the feel of her, had haunted him through the sleepless night and finally driven him back outside; or how he'd spent the hours until dawn sitting under the copper beech, keeping vigil and fending off that other memory of the day the cat got stuck up the tree, and Meredith's legs, graceful as a ballerina's, came down the ladder and caused the seeds of temptation, already implanted in his heart, to flourish.

Chief Myers' pudgy fist reached for the telephone. 'Reckon it's easy enough to find out,' he drawled. 'You're registered as a guest at the hotel, as I recall. Darby Bradford could tell me fast enough what time you picked up your key last night.'

Tom ground his teeth together in frustration. 'I was at the house.'

The squinty eyes gleamed. *'All night?'*

'All night.'

'You have any witnesses to testify to that, too, by any chance?' the Chief asked slyly.

Tom knew an overpowering urge to smash his fist in the older man's meaty face. 'Florence Widdowes made up a bed for me in the TV-room. I left first thing this morning, but she can attest to the fact that the bed had been slept in.'

A pitiful alibi, one Tom had heard a thousand times from men trying to prove their innocence of extra-marital philandering. As legal counsel for betrayed and bitter wives, he had perfected the art of raising one eyebrow in sceptical disbelief of such a flimsy tale.

Chief Myers, who was incapable of such finesse, merely grinned nastily. 'Did you go peeping in any rooms, Thomas Patrick, and getting those ladies all in a twitter?'

Tom felt the blood rush to his head, blurring his vision. 'You disgusting piece of——!' he began, his rage almost boiling over.

'Thinking of punching me out, boy?' Abel Myers taunted.

His eagerness was like a splash of cold water in the face. Suddenly, Tom was entirely in control of himself. He would rather die than give the town the satisfaction of seeing him thrown into jail for assault. 'I want you to file a report, Chief Myers. Now. Or I'll use my legal know-how to have you hauled into court for failing in your duty to protect the citizens of the area.'

Abel Myers' grin faded. 'I don't need the likes of you to tell me my job, Tom Whitney. You'll get your complaint filed, but the next time this...' he leered '...this Peeping *Tom* shows up, you tell Meredith to call me and let the authorities take care of the matter.'

Tom encountered the same attitude everywhere he went. Whether covert or direct, the message remained the same: you're not needed here; get out of town and leave us to take care of our own.

It galled him to be the recipient of such sound advice from people he held in such low esteem, but, whatever else his shortcomings, Tom wasn't stupid. He knew full well that, left to run unhindered, things between him and Meredith would become complicated. He was a man used to setting himself clear goals, and to pursuing them with logical and unswerving devotion—the ultimate yuppie, he acknowledged wryly: relentlessly ambitious and married to success.

There wasn't room in his plans for the likes of Meredith, a woman given to deep emotions and strong personal commitment. They shared nothing in common but a rotting old house. If he sometimes felt differently, it could only be because he was letting himself get side-tracked by lust, and at his age he damned well ought to know better.

He'd stayed in town because he'd thought he could do her a favour. Now it was time to cut the ties that threatened to bind, and do her an even bigger favour by getting out of her life before she found herself ostracised by people whose good

opinion she valued. Already the tongues were
wagging, the rumours flying. And last night he'd
learned that, for all her competence and assurance
in other matters, when it came to affairs of the heart
Meredith was woefully inexperienced.

He'd kissed enough women to know how to
interpret the messages conveyed, the flirtatious
versus the blatantly invitational or the calculatingly
deliberate. Meredith was different, employing
neither artifice nor guile. She wanted to give—but
he was afraid he wasn't ready to receive. He would
hurt her. Better to make it a small hurt from which
she'd recover. Better to leave her with some of her
ideals still intact.

The heat continued unabated for the remainder of
the week after Eleanor found the intruder in the
house, but for some reason Tom slaved as though
driven by something more than the desire to have
the roof patched before the next rainfall. At first,
Meredith thought he was just too busy to socialise,
but, as the days progressed and she caught him
chatting with other members of the family even
though he apparently had no time to spare her more
than a cursory word, she grew suspicious.

When he declined her specific invitation to join
them for a dinner of fried chicken Maryland, which
she happened to know was one of his favourite
dishes, and chose instead to work until well after
dark, she was forced to conclude that he was pur-
posely avoiding her, and she decided she deserved
to know why.

After dinner, she went upstairs and took a long,
cool bath while she waited for the others to finish

their evening activities. She loved her family, but there were times lately that she found herself wishing for more privacy. Finally, with everyone else at last settled for the night, she went searching for Tom, carrying a tray set with a cold supper.

'Union rules insist a man take a break at least once in twelve hours,' she said lightly, timing her arrival to coincide with his packing away the tools he'd used, 'so I brought you something to eat.'

'Thanks, but I'm through for today. I'll just grab a bite down at the hotel.' He nodded as distantly as if they were strangers and, reaching through the open window of the truck, started up the engine.

He seemed oblivious to the fact that she was dressed in something other than the shorts he was accustomed to seeing her wear, that her loose-fitting caftan whispered silkily when she moved and that she smelled of Chanel for a change, instead of paint thinner.

Normally the most straightforward man she'd ever met, he averted his gaze, and she knew at once that he was being evasive with her. 'Isn't that a bit of a waste, considering there's a meal already made and waiting here?'

'Maybe,' he replied, still refusing to look her in the eye, 'but I'll pass just the same. I need a shower in the worst way.'

'We have two bathrooms, both with showers, that you've used other times.'

'Why don't you stop pushing, Meredith?' he snapped irritably.

'Why don't you tell me why you've avoided me all week and don't want to spend time with me now?' She examined his face in the glow from the dashboard lights, taking note of the strain around his eyes, the grim line of his mouth. 'Is it because you kissed me again, and wish now that you hadn't?'

'Oh, hell!' he cursed softly, and looked fully at her for the first time in days. 'Don't you know it isn't fashionable to be so direct? A woman's supposed to be coy about things like that.'

'You told me once that you didn't care for pretence, and I'm not very good at playing games.' Belying the claim, she shrugged with false nonchalance. '*Are* you sorry?'

'Meredith!' He thudded his forehead against the truck door in mock despair. When she continued to survey him patiently, he raised his head. 'No, I'm not sorry,' he admitted reluctantly, 'at least, not in the way you think. I just don't want to make life difficult for you.'

She set the tray down on the veranda steps. 'But you don't! You've made things much easier.'

'Perhaps as far as the house goes, but I'm talking more about...' He jerked his head in the direction of the road. 'About people in town. Gossip, Meredith. As I recall, it always was a major source of entertainment around here, and I don't want to do anything that would leave you its victim.'

'It was just a kiss, Tom.' She smiled at him, denying the little stab of misery the words cost her. 'And I won't tell anyone, if you don't.' The truth was, she'd have been proud to shout out the news for everyone to hear. She'd hardly slept in the nights since for thinking about it, reliving the memory of it over and over again and finding it no less wonderful with each repetition. His subsequent aloofness, however, had caused her considerable pain.

No one had ever affected her like this. The only other man she'd dated before Andrew had been a student she'd known during her university days. His idea of kissing had been so unpleasant, his mouth grinding into hers so brutally, that she had slapped him. Her response had brought a speedy end to a rather unlovely relationship. As for Andrew, he'd been warm and gentle and kind, and at the time that had seemed enough, but now she realised there'd been no fire, no promise, in his love-making. He'd bestowed affection and asked for nothing more in return. Last week, Tom had opened new doors for her and given her a glimpse of a different kind of sharing between a man and a woman.

'What's on the tray?' he asked grudgingly, apparently interpreting her silence as a refusal to go away and leave him in peace.

'Cold chicken, potato salad, watermelon pickles, and cherry tart.'

'I'm weakening,' he confessed. 'Is that a pitcher of cider I see?'

'And two glasses.'

He sighed resignedly and switched off the truck engine. 'The towels——?'

'On the shelf where they always are, and Dolores left your clean laundry on top of the clothes drier.'

'Pour the cider, Meredith. I'll be back in a flash.'

He was gone slightly longer, leaving her to gaze after him thoughtfully. She'd learned long ago to trust her instincts. They were all she'd had to guide her, and they were nagging at her now, telling her to tread boldly. Resolutely, she picked up the tray and took it around to the back porch. She wasn't normally the sort of person to run headlong into danger, but she couldn't erase the feeling that something momentous and irresistibly enticing lay within her grasp, and she knew an overpowering urge to reach out and take it. Some sixth sense told her that if she didn't, she might live with regret the rest of her life.

She knew the minute he came out and joined her, even though he moved silently on bare feet. The scent of her shampoo mingling with the fresh outdoor smell of clothing that had hung in the sun to dry preceded him.

'I guess I was hungrier than I realised,' he said, joining her on the porch swing and making short work of the chicken.

'I'm not surprised. You put in a long day.'

'Yes, well, I'm kind of in a hurry to get finished,' he said.

Her heart leapt unpleasantly at that. 'Why?' she asked, pouring cider with an unsteady hand.

'I've got a law practice waiting for me in Toronto.' Even in the gloom, she knew he was looking straight at her. 'I can't put my life on hold indefinitely, Meredith.'

The feelings that flooded through her at his declaration were not gratitude or regret or acceptance, or any of those sane and civilised things. They were shock and despair and pure, undiluted misery. They were the sort of feelings that a person experienced when she stood in danger of losing someone vital to her happiness. They were the sort of feelings that robbed a person of all pride. 'I don't want you to go,' she said, her voice hollow with a need she'd only just discovered.

Very carefully, he placed his fork on the plate and pushed aside the tray. 'Don't do this, Meredith,' he warned.

'I can't help it. I—*we* all—we'll...miss you.' She floundered, horrified at how close she'd come to saying something quite different and completely unrehearsed: I think I love you, Tom.

'You knew all along that I'd leave eventually.'

'Yes, but I tried not to think about it.'

He swore softly. 'You should be speeding me on my way. Don't you know that a person is judged by the company she keeps? And that, by local standards, you've been displaying some pretty questionable judgement by being seen with me?'

'I don't care about that.' She heard the forlorn tone in her voice and hated herself for her inability to dissemble. How gauche he must find her.

'You should care,' he chided, 'and you will, when those who really matter to you turn their backs on you. You saw what happened the day I rented the truck, Meredith. Do you want to be the target of more of that sort of thing from other people around town?'

I want you! she almost said. For people who professed not to dabble in pretence, she and Tom had wasted a lot of time pretending not to notice the currents flowing between the two of them, but a few nights ago all that had changed. At least, it had for her, and she thought it would be a crime if he were to leave now, without giving them the chance to explore what it was that had crystallised between them.

A three-quarter moon climbed over the trees, etching the strong, clean lines of his face in pewter. He sat half-turned towards her, his dark hair clinging damply to his skull, the shadow of his lashes hiding the thoughts mirrored in his eyes.

She couldn't help reaching out and touching his cheek, feeling the roughness of a day's growth of beard, and wondering how she would deal with the emptiness he'd leave behind when he returned to his real life. 'I suppose you think I'm acting like a fool,' she said shakily. 'Well, if I am, it's all your fault. You were supposed to be miserable and un-feeling. I could have dealt with that, but I wasn't prepared for your kindness and compassion and generosity. I didn't know how brave you were, or how strong.' She sniffed. 'Good grief,' she heard herself admit in a watery little voice, 'I think I might cry.'

His hands closed warmly around hers. 'Meredith,' he begged huskily, 'don't do this to me—to us. I hear what you're really saying, and I can't give you what you want. I don't want to hurt you.'

'What makes you think you will?' she asked, attempting a last feeble stab at courage.

He sighed heavily. 'Because you believe in happy endings, and I don't. I'm not even sure I believe in love, Meredith, any more than I believe...' he scowled, searching for just the right words '...in winter roses.'

'But it's all around you, Tom,' she cried, for-getting to be careful. 'Look at this family, at the way we care for each other, for you.'

'Don't include me in all that! I'm just the landlord doing everyone a favour.'

'Do you really believe it's only gratitude that makes Eleanor dote on you the way she does? And if it is, why do all her pathetic little attempts to please you make you go all soft inside?'

'I most assuredly do not "go all soft inside". That's not my style.'

'I've seen you and heard you. You give her little hugs, show her extra consideration. Why are you like that, Tom, if you think she's just showing gratitude?'

'Shut up, Meredith!'

'I won't. And what about Henry and Prudence? Can you honestly sit here and tell me you don't think they're in love?'

'They're about as rare as winter roses, too.' The breath whistled past his lips in exasperation, and he paused as though choosing his next words with extreme care. 'Look, I'm not denying love in general. I just don't think romantic love, the sort that inspires song writers and poets, has much going for it.'

'Perhaps you think too much,' she said, desperation making her reckless. That tantalising anticipation of something exquisite waiting to be discovered was slipping away, and she couldn't relinquish it without a fight. He'd been the one who'd made her aware that she was settling for half-measures, and now she wanted him to be the one to teach her what it was she'd missed during all those years that she'd believed herself a whole woman.

She slid her hand down his throat and rested her palm on his chest. The sudden acceleration of his heart shot her full of hope. Deliberately, she reached up with her other hand and pulled his head down until his mouth almost touched hers. 'I won't pretend something that feels so right isn't real, Tom,' she whispered.

For a second, she thought he was going to push her away again. She heard his indrawn breath, felt his rejection in the sudden bracing of the muscles beneath her fingers, and she couldn't quite contain a sigh that threatened to dissolve into a sob. That moved him where her other attempts failed.

Choking out a groan, he threaded his fingers through her hair and cupped the back of her head. 'I must be mad,' he murmured against her mouth, then blotted out the moonlight and every last shred of her composure with a kiss that lured her into even more dangerous waters than those she'd encountered the week before.

This time, he didn't stop. He held her firmly against him and explored every inch of her face, from her hairline to the tip of her chin, his mouth seeking out the perfumed hollows beneath her ears and the sleek angle of her cheekbones. Only when he was thoroughly acquainted with all of them did he fasten his lips to hers again with a dedication that paid no heed to reason or sanity.

She felt her limbs grow heavy with desire even as a tension deep within her radiated electricity over every inch of her skin. She wanted him to touch her, wanted to touch him. He aroused longings in her, emotions more potent than anything she had dreamed existed, and she knew that, after tonight, nothing would ever be the same again. Beneath them, the old swing creaked with a rhythm that seemed to punctuate their growing impatience.

His hands drifted over her shoulders, sweeping aside the loose caftan, and she heard the sharp intake of his breath mingle with the whisper of silk as he encountered her nakedness beneath the fabric. Suddenly shy, she blessed the moonlight that filtered over her, turning her breasts to ivory crowned with dark, rich rubies, but hiding the flush that ran up her neck to stain her face. She had never behaved so wantonly in all her life before, and it suddenly seemed very important that he know that.

'I don't...I usually wear...I...' In her agitation, she tried to cover herself. How was it he'd described her, that day in the hotel dining-room?

'Not bad-looking'. The words came back to haunt her with uncompromising fidelity, undermining the courage that had possessed her just moments before. What if she'd misread the signals, and he found her attempt to seduce him a ridiculous charade? What if he went along with it anyway, and found her inadequate? She wasn't voluptuous or sexy, and, although she'd been married, she suddenly didn't feel very experienced, either.

His gaze focused on her face as his hands reached out to capture both hers and draw them away from their protective pose. 'I know. You don't have to explain anything, Meredith,' he said, his voice thick with tenderness. 'Please don't hide yourself from me like this.'

'I don't want you to think...' What? That she hadn't planned this, when they both knew she had?

'I think you're beautiful,' he whispered, pressing kisses to her throat and along her shoulder, 'and very, very desirable.'

His sincerity melted her shyness. Encouraged, she embarked on her own voyage of discovery, trailing her fingers down his ribs and across the washboard strength of his stomach. The results were gratifyingly immediate.

'Meredith,' he muttered urgently, 'I'm not made of stone. Keep that up and there'll be no stopping, no going back.'

'I don't want to stop.' She loved the feel of him, the leashed power, the supple strength; the taste of him, the smell, the texture. He filled her senses more completely than anything she could have imagined.

'No regrets, tomorrow?'

'No regrets.' His skin was flawless, sometimes smooth as heavy satin, sometimes furred with hair that curled around her fingertips as though begging her to prolong the sweet agony of her touch.

He let loose a ragged sigh, and in one fluid movement scooped her into his arms and rose to his feet. 'Not here,' he said, 'and not inside... I don't want an audience.'

'The garden,' she murmured against his shoulder, even as he swung down the steps and across the lawn, stopping at last under the trees next to where the creek burbled musically on its journey to the river. The night air was so still that not even the cottonwoods sighed, and the shadows beneath them lay black and concealing as a cave.

His mouth closed on hers again, savouring her softness. The caftan slithered down around her ankles, leaving the grass cool against her bare skin.

His touch explored the length of her, lingering on the creamy smoothness of her inner thigh, the dim arabesque of her hip, the slender parenthesis of her waist.

Independent of conscious will, her hands took on a life of their own, at once frenzied and nimble as they attacked the barriers that separated him from her. A button tore softly loose from his shirt, the buckle at his waist snapped free. She wanted to feel him naked against her, heart to heart, limb to limb. She wanted him to possess her and never let her go, and if that was asking for too much, then she wanted at least to take a part of him and keep it with her forever.

He knew. Dragging his mouth away from missions more intimate than anything she'd ever anticipated, he towered above her, the whole of him gathered in taut concentration. For the space of a second, perhaps two, she could have saved herself, could have flung aside desire and turned her back on knowledge; gone to her grave without ever having fully lived and never known what she'd missed.

And then it was too late. With a driving, primitive strength, he lost himself in her, and taught her that what she thought she'd known of love was but a pale imitation of the real thing.

Instinctively, she closed around him, provoking in him a response that left them both shaking. The slow-burning heat of his seduction exploded into a raging fire that left restraint lagging pitifully behind passion. Meredith clung to him, the lazy twirling sensations inside that had mesmerised her gather-

ing momentum until she was spinning, out of
control and terrified she was going to fly apart.

'Tom!' she cried, her voice thready and distant
in her ears.

His arms tightened around her, but he couldn't
save her. Nothing could. She'd stepped off the edge
of the world as she knew it, into a thundering and
endless space. All he could do was stay with her,
hurtling towards that same, alien destination, as
shaken and helpless as she.

She thought he might have spoken, might have
cried out something wild and unintelligible to her,
but she was too consumed with the raw emotions
laid bare by the passion exploding through her.
Knowledge, fearsome and merciless, licked over her,
salt on the exposed wounds of her discovery.

She knew now what it was that had been missing
from her life. She could put a name to what it was
she'd yearned for in her lonely bed. It was something she'd never known before, and as different
from what she'd shared with Andrew as night from
day. There was nothing easy about this new
emotion; nothing comfortable, nothing mild. It was
harsh and fierce and exquisite, demanding and
taking without leave or consent, and caring not at
all if she was strong enough to survive its on-
slaught. And just because Tom said he didn't believe in it, it didn't make it any less valid for her.
Or any less magnificent.

Eventually, and with great reluctance, Meredith
admitted the real world again. The sound of the
creek intruded, the first intimation that she she was
still alive and in familiar surroundings. Gradually,
she became aware of other sounds: an owl's eerie

call, the chirp of unseen cicadas, and the decreasing drumroll of her own heart.

She became aware of the grass, fragrant and faintly chill against her overheated skin, and a shiver rippled over her. Tom stirred, lifted his head and looked down at her, his eyes fathomless shadows in the night. 'You're cold,' he murmured, stroking back the hair from her face.

'No,' she protested, unwilling to forfeit the close familiarity of his body over hers, but he was reaching for the caftan, handing it to her, and slipping into his own clothes with a haste that suggested already he regretted what had transpired between them. 'Tom? Are you...?'

He forestalled the question. 'No regrets, remember?' He rose to his feet and held out a hand. 'Get up, sweetheart. You can't lie here all night. Bill would have a stroke if he found you when he comes out to check his tomatoes in the morning.'

But Bill's feelings weren't paramount in Meredith's mind just then. 'What about you?' she asked. 'How do you feel, Tom?'

CHAPTER SEVEN

TOM CONSIDERED the question for a moment. 'Overawed would be a good word. Dazzled, perhaps. Stunned.' He shrugged and laughed quietly. 'Thirsty! How's that for a more prosaic response? Do you suppose there's any more cider in that pitcher?'

She took his outstretched hand and rose gracefully to her feet, pride stepping in to rescue her. It told her not to think, because, if she did, disappointment would clamour to be heard, despair would rush in close behind, and then words would spill out and make her sound pathetic. Whatever else, she would not whine or beg. She would not.

Picking up the caftan, she raised it over her head, let the fabric slip down to cover her all the way to her ankles, and adjusted the V neckline. 'If there isn't, I know where we can find more.'

'Actually,' he said, his voice suddenly rough as sandpaper, 'I think maybe I'll just head out of here.' He glanced up at the moon which had sunk below the trees to cast long, bright shadows over the house. 'It must be close to midnight and I want to get a lot done tomorrow.'

Hope refused to die. With me? she wanted to ask.

Don't cling now, Meredith! She bit her lip to keep silent and failed. 'Anything special?' she enquired, and shrivelled inside at the desperation she heard in her voice.

As they talked, they strolled back to where he'd parked the truck on what had once been the service entrance at the side of the house. Unlike the imposing front driveway, this was just a short paved stretch that led out to the road through a single wrought-iron gate. Quickly, he opened the truck door and, with one foot already inside, turned to look back at her over his shoulder. 'A few boards on the front veranda, and a section of railing near the steps, then I'm done.'

She couldn't help the dismay that she knew filled her eyes. He saw it, too, and pulled her to him. 'Oh, Meredith,' he murmured roughly, 'please don't look at me like that.'

'Like what?' she asked, drawing on every last ounce of courage she possessed not to burst into tears and beg him to stay.

'Like a flower that I just ground under my heel,' he replied, and buried his face in her hair.

Somewhere out of sight, leaves rustled and a moment later, just beyond the laurel hedge that screened them from the road, an engine roared into life and raced away into the night.

'Oh, damn!' Tom cursed, casting her off and spinning around.

'Who was it?' Meredith craned her neck to see past him. 'Did you recognise him?'

Tom shook his head in disgust. 'No, but you can be sure he recognised us.'

'You mean someone was spying on us?' Meredith shivered at the idea, then felt heat rush through her at the thought of all an observer might have witnessed.

'I rather think it was Eleanor's prowler, back to see what sort of fresh mischief he could stir up. I'm sure he didn't expect to find us.' Tom's tone was savage. 'I bet he thinks he really hit pay dirt this time.'

'What do you mean?'

He looked at her, Meredith thought, as though she tried every last vestige of his patience. 'Grow up, Meredith! You can bet he isn't going to keep this little morsel of gossip to himself.'

What a voracious appetite for punishment love gave a person, she decided, crushed that Tom could so easily dismiss the most momentous experience of her life as nothing but 'a little morsel of gossip', that he was so willing to relegate her feelings to the level of a child's. 'I can't imagine anyone being so crass as to broadcast it around town,' she said.

Tom laughed unkindly. 'Then you're even more naïve than I thought, but for your sake I hope that this time you're right.'

She was wrong, as she discovered the minute she showed up at the Town Square grocer's the next morning. A small crowd had gathered outside its open doorway, customers some of them, and others people passing by or from neighbouring business establishments. Josh Hartley was there and so was Cal Gibson.

The hum of conversation dribbled into silence at her approach, and for every pair of eyes that burned accusingly at her she was conscious of another that turned furtively away, pretending not to see her. It was as though she'd barged in on some very private meeting to which she was most emphatically not invited.

Refusing to be intimidated by the covert antagonism, she set about her shopping, and gradually the voices struck up again, raised just high enough that she could hear the words. The oblique references followed her inside the store as she picked up items from the list Florence had made out and dropped them in her shopping cart.

'No sense of fitness. Or shame.'

'...how could she? And with him of all people...'

'You'd think, after being married to a decent man...'

'Disrespectful, I'd call it.'

'Brazen, more like.'

Coming on top of everything else, it was suddenly too much. 'If you have something that you'd like to get off your chests,' Meredith declared, swinging her cart around and confronting the group now congregated near the check-out counter, 'at least be good enough to say it plainly and to my face.'

There was another silence, this one rife with hostility. Then a voice rang out. 'Is it true, then, that you're ... *keeping company* with Tom Whitney?'

The little pause left hanging halfway through the question, the subtle emphasis that turned a harmless phrase offensive, told Meredith plainly enough that last night's spy had lost no time in spreading graphic rumours. 'Who told you that?' she asked sharply.

The faces that had once welcomed her so openly closed against her now. 'Is it true?' another voice persisted.

'What if it is?' she shot back. 'I'm not breaking any laws.'

'You're Andrew Blake's widow,' Josh Hartley said, pushing himself to the forefront of the group. 'When you came to me that day and asked me to run your story in the *Times*, I thought that meant something to you, Meredith.' He shook his head. 'I don't know how you can sleep nights, knowing you're defiling his memory like this.'

'Andrew's been dead almost four years,' Meredith said. 'How long am I supposed to stay in mourning?'

'Oh, child!' Len Mackie's wife reproved her softly. 'It's not that we think you shouldn't live your life—but with a man like Tom Whitney?' She shook her head sadly.

There it was again, the intimation that, despite her age, Meredith was not adult enough to fully understand life or take charge of her own affairs. Was it something she'd brought on herself? Was she still looking for the parents she'd always wanted and encouraging others to assume those roles, as Tom had accused over lunch that day? And if so, how did she now put a stop to it? Because there was no doubt that, some time over the course of the summer, she'd grown up. She no longer required parental approval. Her needs were different now, more complex and less easily satisfied.

She flung out both hands, palms up. 'I don't understand your resentment,' she said. 'What did Tom do that was so bad that no one can forgive him? He left here when he was just seventeen. How much trouble can a boy that age cause?'

Josh Hartley's face turned dark with suppressed rage. 'Plenty,' he growled. 'You don't know the half of it.'

'Then tell me the rest,' she cried, 'instead of all standing there like hanging judges! Why do *you* hate him so much, Josh?'

'Don't rake up old scandals, girl,' Cal Gibson warned. 'Some wounds never heal.'

They were inflexible in their hatred of Tom, and it didn't make sense. She knew they weren't normally cruel people. They'd been so kind to her, so approving. What had he done to incur such lasting condemnation?

'Well, it seems as though you have no answers,' she said into the waiting silence.

'Seems you don't much value our opinions any more,' Cal replied. 'There was a time, Meredith, when what we thought mattered a lot to you. In fact, there was a time when you couldn't rightly have got along without us.'

That was true, Meredith conceded privately. There had been a time when the support and good will of every resident in this town had boosted her sense of self-worth, just as there'd been a time when the security and affection she'd known in her marriage to Andrew had satisfied all her more personal needs. But that was before Tom had come along and she'd discovered there could be more to a relationship between a man and a woman; that there could be passion and desire which, once awakened, were not easily dismissed. They made what she'd known before pale by comparison.

The residents of Riverbridge were essentially good people, and they meant well. They had stood behind her when she'd had no one else to turn to, but she'd made it easy for them, she realised with belated insight. She'd conformed to their way of doing things. She'd been a good wife to a man they'd all respected and admired, but, more than that, she'd been an exemplary widow. She had always been predictably conservative, and for her to settle her affections on a man like Tom was, to their way of thinking, to show a conspicuous lack of mature judgement. It seemed they'd rather she let her youth slip away and face old age alone. She was halfway there already, nicely settled in a home for seniors, with nothing but a handful of tepid memories to keep her warm at night.

She stacked her purchases on the counter and waited until the amount she owed had been rung up on the cash register before turning again to the group surrounding her. 'I'm sorry if what I'm about to say upsets you,' she said with a calmness that amazed even her. 'You must know how much I value your good opinion. This town is home to me, even though I have no real family here as such, and it's thanks to all of you that I feel that way. You were my friends when I needed you the most.'

She paused and drew in a deep breath, knowing that what she was about to say next might make her as much an outcast as Tom, but knowing also that, in the final analysis, she had to set her own values on life and abide by her own concepts of morality. Of all the things she was experiencing, shame and regret were the least of her emotions. She could not live with herself if she took the easy route now, and denied those feelings which had finally freed her and allowed her to become a woman in the truest sense of the word. Last night she'd been half afraid to admit the truth, but, now that she'd been forced to confront it, she would not back away from it.

'I love Tom Whitney,' she said, and in the silence that followed it seemed as though a person could hear the dust motes dancing in the sunbeams. No one but she noticed that another person had stepped into the doorway of the store in time to hear her declaration. No one else saw the expression on his face as the impact of her words sank home. But she saw, and she thought she would carry with her to her grave the memory of the utter horror in those brilliant blue eyes of his. In that moment she feared that she'd left herself teetering on a precipice without a hope in the world of saving herself from falling over its edge.

Then pandemonium erupted.

'Love that swine?' Josh Hartley was livid. 'It's as well you don't have family, Meredith Blake, because hearing that would be enough to make them wish they didn't own you!'

'How would you know?' she shot back, devastated to find that, when her back was to the wall, she could be as cruel as the next person. 'You don't have family, either!'

'But I did,' he roared, anguish breaking his voice. 'I had a daughter just like you, and I had a wife, too, and he killed them both!'

Meredith clapped a hand to her mouth. 'That's not true!' she gasped, not sure which she was denying: the daughter, the wife, or the accusation.

'It is true,' Josh bellowed, beside himself with pain. 'As I'm standing here, it's the absolute truth!'

They were all watching her, waiting for her to recognise the error of her ways and denounce the man she professed to love, but she felt suspended in time, her next breath stillborn and only her eyes, fixed on Tom's face, begging for the response that would end this nightmare.

Defend yourself! her heart cried out. Tell me they're wrong. Don't make me face them alone.

He stood there, a good six inches taller than any other man present, poised in the doorway, the sleek, elegant muscles tense, the stance wary and defensive. She saw the proud tilt of his head, the arrogant blue stare, the handsome, withdrawn face. There was no trace of tenderness, no hint of remorse or regret, no indication of the fiery passion that she'd seen him tame to gentleness with Eleanor. His features were deliberately expressionless, as empty as the seconds stringing out the silence. And then, when she thought she'd snap in two from the tension, he moved at last and, without a word, turned and walked away.

If he had slapped her, she could not have felt more shocked or humiliated. It was small enough consolation to know that none of the rest of them had been aware of his presence, that they mistook her sudden pallor for distress at Josh's allegations.

'It was a long time ago, Meredith . . .'

'No one talks about it any more. You couldn't have known.'

'. . . but we've never forgotten . . .'

Like a sleep-walker, Meredith folded her receipt, placed it carefully in her purse, and gathered up the sack of groceries. 'I must go now,' she said, her voice echoing strangely in her ears. The blood rushed through her veins, racing to keep the life-force vital and strong, as though it knew that her heart felt too crushed to go on beating.

She didn't care what Tom had done in the past, whether or not the accusations were valid. Life was the present, and hope was what made the future. And that look she'd brought to his eyes with her proud, impetuous declaration told her with merciless cruelty what he'd tried to say kindly the night before: he did not wish to share either today or tomorrow with her.

The present ended as suddenly as it had begun. Within hours, he was gone. She didn't need to be told that the truck he'd rented had been returned to Cal Gibson's yard, its keys left in the ignition. She didn't need to check at the hotel to find he was no longer registered there. She knew all those things because, even though the sunlight continued to pour through the windows of the Whitney house, it couldn't stave off the coldness around her heart, or warm the pale, pinched features of her face to rosy life. As for the future, it ceased to be of consequence. Memories were all that endured, all that mattered, after all.

The aircraft was half empty, and Tom had both seats on the window aisle to himself. Within minutes of take-off, he was able to recline his seat as far as possible and stretch himself across space normally reserved for two passengers. The hostess was leggy and lovely. She poured his Scotch just the way he liked it, lightly bruised with ice, and made sure he had an extra pillow. He was headed back where he belonged, and every passing minute put more miles

between him and a place so small it didn't even rate
a mention on the map. All that he had left to do
was bury the remembrance of a summer liaison so
fleeting that already it had assumed the nebulous
unreality of a dream.

He shifted to a more comfortable position,
adjusted the seat once again and reached for the
financial magazine left behind by a previous trav-
eller. The Toronto stock market was up, his port-
folio healthier than when he'd left it. Property was
once more on the rise. And Meredith's face kept
interposing itself between him and the printed page.

Guilt, he decided. That was all it was, and if it
left him feeling uncomfortable he deserved it. He
should never have allowed things to run out of
control the way they had. Damn it, he was experienced enough to know that, for a woman like
Meredith, sex involved a lot more than a purely
physical exchange.

Of course, she didn't really love him. It was just
her way of justifying what had happened. It
wouldn't take long for her to realise that they were
about as mismatched as a couple could possibly be,
and that she'd be far better off with someone who
shared her small-town contentment.

As for himself, he didn't need or want the com-
plications she represented. He'd gone back to the
town to liquidate his assets and sever the last
remaining ties, not to form new attachments, and
definitely not to break hearts. Just because her face
haunted him right now, it didn't alter his overall
plan. He knew himself too well.

He was ambitious, he was bright, he knew where
he was going and what he wanted, and it didn't

involve anything to do with Riverbridge or a curly-haired ballerina of a woman who came saddled with a houseful of old folks. He had his sights set on bigger things. He wanted the stimulation and the glamour that only a big-city law practice could provide; the high-profile court cases, the professional respect, the front-page exposure. Most of all, he wanted the freedom to go where his spirit beckoned.

In a month or two, Meredith would have forgotten he'd ever happened. Once everyone realised he was gone for good, they'd overlook her lapse and things would go on as usual. And, just to make sure of that, he'd never go back there again. When the house lease expired next year, Reginald Swabey could look after things. That was what he got paid for.

Oh, Tom supposed right now that she hated him for running out on her the way he had, and if he was really honest he'd admit it bothered him, too. He hadn't planned to leave so abruptly, but she'd more or less forced his hand and, all things considered, this way was probably the best.

The bottom line was that, whether the locals wanted to believe it or not, he was no longer the careless individual of his teenage years. He had a conscience and his own personal code of ethics, and he wasn't about to expose Meredith to further censure or hurt by prolonging an affair which was fated to end with summer. That was why he hadn't waited to explain himself to her. If it would make it a little easier for her to accept his defection by believing that what Josh Hartley had alleged was the literal truth, then who was Tom Whitney to deprive her of comfort with technicalities? A swift, clean break was best. No protracted farewells, no explanations, no excuses.

No regrets. Her voice echoed through his mind, and he felt a pain somewhere near his heart. Her face swirled into focus again, the sweet mouth, the soft grey eyes.

The hostess paused in the aisle beside him. '*Filet mignon* or crab, sir?'

'What's your recommendation?'

Her smile was an invitation. 'That depends on how hungry you are.'

Suddenly, he felt very jaded and very depressed. 'I don't have much appetite for anything. Bring me another Scotch, then don't disturb me again until we're ready to land.'

Meredith hated the nights, the long, dark hours when the memories hung so brightly in her mind's eye, but she hated the days more. The overt we-told-you-so pity she received from some people around town was hard enough to take, but the unspoken commiseration and hushed tact from others she found unbearable.

The family were wonderful. Prudence extended unlimited tea and uncritical sympathy. Florence said little but spent a lot of time in the kitchen baking special treats to tempt Meredith's failing appetite.

Lucille, surprisingly, offered the most solid comfort. 'One tends to believe,' she announced, with a faraway look in her eyes completely at odds with her down-to-earth tone, 'that hearts break when a person is disappointed in love, but that simply isn't true. We are much stronger than we suspect, my dear Meredith, and if there is one thing I have learned, it is that, as long as there is life, there is always hope for tomorrow. Thomas has made a mistake, and there is nothing you can do to rectify that except be patient and hope he comes to see the error of his ways before it is too late.'

Dolores proved an unexpected ally. 'Listen to Lucille,' she counselled Meredith. 'She's absolutely right. Everything will work out. I've seen it all in the leaves.' And, for once, Lucille did not repudiate the claim.

At first, Meredith continued to hope. She sat by the telephone, waiting for a call that never came. Then she watched for the postman, practically snatching his deliveries out of his hand and riffling through the envelopes, looking for one with a Toronto postmark that also never came. Finally, as the lazy days of August slid into golden September, she accepted that Tom wasn't going to contact her again; that the most she would get in the way of explanations were the details Bill supplied to flesh out Josh's startling revelation.

'It was a tragedy,' he began, one evening when everyone but Eleanor, who had gone to bed early, gathered on the veranda after dinner to enjoy what was left of summer, 'and Tom Whitney was right in the middle of it. He'd been in trouble since he was old enough to walk, and by the time he was a senior in high school he was as lawless and arrogant as they come, and too handsome for his own good. The Hartleys had a daughter, Fiona, the apple of Josh's eye, and when Tom left town she followed him. She'd had a crush on him for months, and people were beginning to talk; she made such a fool of herself over the boy.'

And they were talking again, Meredith thought bitterly, except that this time the object of their gossip wasn't a teenager. Fiona had been only sixteen, but what excuse had she, a grown woman of thirty, to account for her actions?

Bill paused long enough to get his pipe going, then picked up the story again. 'Well, that was the last straw for Josh, and when Rita, his wife, begged him to go after the girl and bring her back home, he point-blank refused. Said she'd made her choice, and she'd have to live with it. So Rita went instead, and on the way back to Riverbridge mother and daughter were killed in a car accident, coming through one of the mountain passes.'

'Then it was hardly Thomas's fault,' Lucille maintained, 'so why did everyone make him the scapegoat?'

'When something like that happens, it seems that people need somebody to blame, and they felt too sorry for Josh to point the finger at him. The grief and the guilt almost destroyed him as it was. The shock of the tragedy rocked this town like nothing I've known before or since, and Tom Whitney left himself wide open as a target. Once again, he'd caused trouble, and what made it worse was that he didn't even have the decency to come back for the funerals. He flaunted his disrespect in everyone's faces, got off scot-free, and left other people to pick up the pieces, just the way he has again with you, Meredith.'

Bill shook his head and sighed. 'I didn't understand the boy, and I don't pretend to understand the man, either. It isn't natural for a person to be so unfeeling.'

But it all made a sad kind of sense to Meredith, who'd seen the other side of Tom. Too late she realised that he didn't know how to deal with love of any kind. Now, all she could do was accept that, put on a brave front and get through the days the best way she knew how.

Unfortunately, Eleanor was not able to do the same. 'She's pining,' Dolores said one day, watching her make her listless way down the drive to the road. 'All she ever asks is when Tommy is coming home again. For some reason, she took a real shine to him.'

Meredith agreed. For her, the onset of autumn brought with it a sort of emotional limbo that dulled the pain of those first weeks after Tom left, and she realised that Lucille was right. She was going to survive, despite the heartache. She knew there'd never be another love like Tom, but she was grateful for what they had shared. She felt richer for the experience and, if she had one lasting regret, it was that Eleanor could not make the same claim.

Meredith could understand Tom's bitterness towards his parents, his resentment of the outsiders who judged him so harshly without ever really knowing the sort of life he'd had as a child, and the pride which prevented him from clearing himself of Josh Hartley's accusations. But his callousness towards a harmless old lady who had loved him simply for himself and asked nothing in return was something Meredith found hard to overlook.

As the leaves on the trees turned scarlet, Eleanor grew more wraithlike and absent-minded than ever, drifting through the days in a world of her own. But she seemed to take pleasure in walking in the park and watching the children play. Meredith hoped, as the days grew shorter, that the upheavals Tom had brought into their lives might fade, and that things might finally settle back to normal for everyone, at least on the surface.

Bill put the garden to bed for the winter and Henry helped him fill the log baskets on the hearths. It was that time of year that drew families together, a time for companionship and cosy evenings spent around the fire.

As long as she didn't allow herself to remember the summer, Meredith was almost happy. Until the week before Thanksgiving, when Eleanor got herself arrested.

CHAPTER EIGHT

THE Friday afternoon he ripped Burton Stokes's testimony to shreds and won Marguerite Stokes a ten-million-dollar matrimonial settlement from her estranged husband should have been an occasion for celebration. But when Tom walked out of court feeling neither elation nor pride at having performed brilliantly in one of those most vitriolic and notorious divorces of the decade, he decided that he could not continue to crusade on behalf of other emotionally fragile people until he had somehow dealt with his own woes.

Turning his back on the television cameras and reporters waiting to interview him, he slipped out of a side entrance of the downtown Toronto courthouse and into a taxi, directing the driver to take him back to his apartment. Upon arriving, he ignored the messages on his answering machine, poured himself a stiff drink, and contemplated the future with a disfavour which would have struck him as unthinkable four months earlier.

He ought to be a happy man. Victory in the Stokes case and the offer of a partnership with Finlay, Black and Puckingham, Toronto's most élite firm of lawyers, had coincided to give him the prominence he'd always thought he craved. Even now, champagne glasses were clinking in his honour at a party in a suite of the Royal York Hotel, the guests as yet unaware that he had decided not to attend because his life suddenly seemed empty of anything worth celebrating.

They'd no doubt howl with well-bred laughter if they knew that, instead of being part of the sophisticated gathering, Tom Whitney was holed up in his apartment, feeling more than a little disgusted with his cut-throat performance in court that afternoon. He ought to be feeling differently. He ought to be exchanging slick repartee and confidential anecdotes with colleagues, flirting politely with their wives, and dangerously with their daughters. He ought not to be thinking of a soft-eyed woman with curly hair who would never, in a million years, understand or condone the values which governed his life.

He ought to be able to look himself in the eye each morning when he shaved. He ought to be able to live with himself.

'Oh, hell!' he cursed, and for perhaps the fiftieth time since August he lifted the phone. This time, however, he dialled the long-distance number and didn't hang up before it could ring at the other end.

'Shoplifting?' Lucille's eyebrows rose disbelievingly. 'Good heavens, man, you've lost your senses. Mrs Kennedy is forgetful, vague and dithery, but she is not a common thief. Apologise to her at once!'

'Sorry, Mrs Delong, but I'm afraid I can't do that. The merchandise was found in her bag, and there is a witness who saw her put it there.'

Refusing to be impressed or cowed by the presence of a uniformed officer of the law in their living-room, Lucille fixed Chief Myers with an imperious glare, apparently prepared to defy God and man rather than allow Eleanor to be subjected to the indignity of prosecution. 'Witness? What witness?'

'Steven Myers, my grandson.'

'Piffle!' Lucille waved a dismissive hand. 'I've seen that grandson of yours slinking around town. How could he possibly witness anything, with all that hair hanging in his face the way it does? He needs to pay a visit to a good barber.'

'That may well be, ma'am, but it doesn't alter the fact that certain items were retrieved from Mrs Kennedy's bag.' Chief Myers consulted his notebook. 'Let's see: a quantity of chocolate bars, a pack of transistor radio batteries, two disposable lighters, a tape recording by a singer named...' he checked the notebook again '...Billy Ocean.'

'Aha!' Lucille crowed triumphantly. 'There's the proof that she's not guilty! What would a woman like Eleanor want with items like those?'

'Shoplifters don't necessarily take that into account, ma'am, and since the lady can't offer any reason for being found in possession, as it were, there's nothing to prevent the management from laying charges against her. And I don't mind telling you,' he went on, overriding Lucille's next objection before it could be uttered, 'that I'm urging him to do so. Over the last six months, he's lost a small fortune in merchandise to this sort of activity, and he can't afford to go on ignoring it.'

'So you plan to make an example of an old lady of seventy-nine?' Meredith protested. 'I can't believe you'd hold her up to public shame and embarrassment for an incident which, at worst, can only be attributed to confusion. You saw the state she was in when you brought her home. She barely knew what was happening or where she was.'

'I don't make the laws, Meredith,' Chief Myers replied heavily. 'I just enforce them.'

Lucille snorted. 'What were those immortal words of Dickens?' she began. '"The law, Mr Bumble, is an——"'

'Never mind,' Meredith interrupted hastily. The situation was bad enough, without Lucille making matters worse, however good her intentions.

It was the Friday before Thanksgiving and Meredith had been determined to make this a happy holiday for the family. She'd shed enough private tears over Tom Whitney, and wasted enough time on futile wishes. Eleanor had finally begun to take a more lively interest in things around her, and her courage had shamed Meredith into pulling herself together, too. For this shoplifting incident to occur at all was a minor tragedy that verged on calamity considering the central figure involved, and would likely cause a terrible set-back for Eleanor. 'What's going to happen, Chief Myers?'

'Mrs Kennedy'll have to go before the magistrate. Since it's her first offence, she'll likely just be fined.'

'She'll have to be found guilty first,' Dolores said tartly, coming into the room in time to hear the Chief's words. 'I just put her to bed and we had a talk. She no more took those things than you did, Abel Myers.'

'I see.' Clearly out of patience, the officer snapped closed his notebook, picked up his cap and rose to leave. 'Did she tell you how they came to be found in her bag, by any chance?'

'She doesn't know.'

'No doubt they jumped in there all on their own, then,' he sneered. 'Good afternoon, ladies. You'll be informed when the court date comes up.'

'I don't like that man,' Dolores said, as the police car swept down the drive and out to the road. 'He gives me the willies.'

'He's a bully,' Lucille announced, 'and poor benighted Eleanor is exactly the sort of victim he likes to pick on.'

Bill and Henry came up from the cellar at that moment, looking perplexed. 'I could have sworn I had another case of Bordeaux put by,' Henry said, 'and I don't remember us using up the last of the Cabernet, either.'

'Well, things have been moved around a bit down there. Maybe, with all those empty boxes lying around, you got mixed up,' Bill suggested.

'No.' Henry was adamant. 'The bottled wine goes in the racks. I have every batch numbered, and I keep accurate records. You saw my lists, Bill.'

'Then I reckon people must've been helping themselves,' Bill cackled. 'Better own up, ladies. Which one of you's been tippling?'

'I may not be entirely perfect,' Lucille informed him haughtily, 'but secret drinking is not one of my vices, and I'll thank you not to be so insulting.'

'I was joking,' Bill muttered, belatedly sensing the gloom in the atmosphere. 'What's got everyone in such a sour mood?'

'And where's Prudence?' Henry wanted to know.

'Upstairs looking after Eleanor,' Dolores said.

'Eleanor's room is down here. Why is she upstairs?'

'I've moved her in with me for a while,' Dolores explained. 'She shouldn't be left by herself too much right now.'

Henry and Bill exchanged mystified glances. 'Is she ill?'

Lucille clicked her tongue impatiently. 'Stop beating around the bush, woman,' she said shortly to Dolores, and turned to the men. 'Eleanor's been arrested for shoplifting in Ryan's General Store, and a more ludicrous tale I have yet to hear.'

'How come you're so thick with Eleanor all of a sudden?' Bill asked, raising his voice over the faint murmur of agreement created by her words and the ringing of the phone in the front hall. 'Seems to me you seldom have much patience with her.'

Lucille sat, spine erect as a débutante's, and surveyed the expectant faces confronting her. 'Eleanor is an absent-minded old fool given to vivid imaginings, but she is not a thief and she is most certainly not a criminal. I can't speak for the rest of you, but I will not stand by and see her bullied into confessing to something she did not do,' she pronounced, then snapped, 'And will someone for heaven's sake answer that telephone? Or are you all suddenly struck deaf as well as spineless?'

'I'll get it,' Florence said, poking her head in the room. 'Dinner's on the table, so call a truce and come and sit down. We can talk about what to do later. We all think better on a full stomach.'

While the others assembled in the dining-room, Meredith took up a tray to Eleanor and tried to coax her to eat, without success. Huddled in the bed, her thin hands with their tracery of blue veins clutching at the covers, Eleanor fixed wide, terrified eyes on Meredith's face. 'I didn't . . .' she began in a quavering voice.

'I know you didn't, darling,' Meredith assured her. 'Please, Eleanor, try to eat a little. I don't want you to get sick.'

But it was as if she had retreated into another world. Nothing Meredith could say, neither promises nor reassurances, made any impression. Eleanor simply turned her face to the wall and would not be reached.

Frustrated, Meredith left a glass of milk by the bed, turned off all but one lamp, and decided that if things hadn't improved by the morning she'd call in the doctor. Regardless, she wasn't about to stand idly by and see Eleanor put through the misery and humiliation of a magistrate's hearing. For once, she and Lucille were in full agreement on something.

Conversation came to an abrupt halt when she reappeared in the dining-room, and everyone became suddenly engrossed with the food on their plates. 'What are you all up to?' she asked, attempting to lighten the mood a little. 'You remind me of children caught with your hands in the cookie jar.'

'We're worried about Eleanor,' Lucille supplied, and glared defiantly around the table. 'Aren't we?'

'Of course!'

'We were just talking about——'

'A formal protest. We'll all go down to the police station in the morning.'

Everyone answered at once. At any other time, their nervousness would have made Meredith extremely suspicious, but she knew how frail their confidence was when anything unforeseen happened. Each one nursed a terrible dread of being left to cope alone in times of difficulty, and she certainly understood why. Who was there to care what happened to them, if they didn't all look out for each other?

'We thought we'd get a lawyer,' Prudence began, then spilled gravy on her blouse as all heads turned to fix her in a warning stare.

'Someone give her a napkin before she spills more than her food,' Lucille suggested waspishly.

'Never mind, precious,' Henry murmured. 'We know you're just upset for Eleanor. We all are.'

'There's lemon meringue pie for dessert,' Florence said, obviously trying to divert attention. 'Why don't we have it in the living-room in front of the fire?'

'And Dolores could read the leaves for us afterwards,' Lucille put in slyly. 'Who knows what we might all learn?'

Meredith got the distinct impression that they were nursing a secret they were not prepared to share with her.

'Hmm...very interesting,' Dolores intoned dramatically, gazing intently at the swirl of leaves in the bottom of Meredith's cup an hour later. 'I see great upheaval...changes, much happiness after great sorrow.'

Prudence started to giggle, prompting Florence to drain her own cup hurriedly and hand it over to Dolores. 'Tell me what you see in mine,' she said.

Dolores sucked in an awed breath. 'A creation coming out of the kitchen,' she whispered. 'Something tall and white and magnificent!'

'A handsome old man, perhaps,' Lucille snickered. 'What about mine?'

'You don't believe in the leaves,' Bill pointed out.

To Meredith's utter surprise, Lucille reached over and slapped him playfully on the wrist. 'I do today,' she retorted with a gleam in her eye. 'What do you see, Dolores?'

'Great activity,' Dolores said obligingly. 'Many flowers, rice . . . organ music—and a big blue hat to match your hair.'

Lucille scowled at the eruption of laughter that produced. 'Very funny, I'm sure!'

'Listen,' Meredith said, glad that the afternoon's misfortune hadn't dampened their holiday spirits, but too concerned about the other member of the family, alone in her bed upstairs, to forget that they had a problem to solve, 'this is all very entertaining, but I think we should decide what we're going to do about Eleanor. Prudence mentioned a lawyer, and of course we must hire one. Who do you suggest? Reginald Swabey, perhaps?'

Florence shook her head. 'He's respected enough that people listen to what he has to say,' she said, 'but he's not very forceful. I think we need someone with more energy.'

'Someone who'll stand up to Abel Myers,' Bill put in. 'Reginald Swabey lets people push him around too much.'

Dolores nodded. 'And Abel Myers is a bully, as we already know.'

'Then who do you suggest?' Meredith asked. 'There isn't a lot of choice in Riverbridge, and I'm concerned.'

'We know that, Meredith,' Henry said, 'but we're all worried about you, too. You look so tired. Why don't we forget all about this until after the weekend? There's nothing we can do anyway until Tuesday, with Monday being a holiday, and by then, who knows what might turn up?'

'An excellent idea, Henry.' Lucille picked up the cups and saucers and piled them on the tray. 'Stop gazing at him as if he's Albert Einstein reborn, Prudence, and help me load these in the dishwasher. As for you, Meredith, go to bed. You look like death warmed over, and it's most unattractive. You want to look your best for tomorrow.'

'Why?' Meredith enquired, a little dazed at Lucille's sudden willingness to help with the dishes, and more than a little suspicious.

For a moment, Lucille looked taken aback. 'Well, it's Thanksgiving weekend,' she stammered. 'I mean . . . well . . .'

'I do believe Lucille's at a loss for words,' Florence chuckled, promoting a fresh outburst of laughter.

It was only after Meredith was in bed that it occurred to her that Lucille hadn't answered her question and that there had been an undercurrent of excitement in the air that evening not normally induced by the prospect of a turkey dinner. Something was definitely afoot.

She found out what it was late the following afternoon when she returned from getting her hair cut. The weather was foul, bringing the day to an early close and she noticed, as she drove up to the house, how warm and cosy it looked with lamp-light gleaming in the windows and smoke curling up from the chimneys.

'You've got a visitor waiting to see you,' Florence greeted her at the back door, and pointed down the hall towards the living-room. 'In there.'

Meredith shook the rain from her coat, hung it up to dry, and tucked her peach-coloured blouse more neatly into the waist of her tailored black trousers. 'Who is it?'

Florence shrugged. 'I think it might have some-thing to do with Eleanor and what happened yes-terday,' she said evasively, and went back to making the dressing for the turkey. Neither Dolores, who was rolling out the pastry for the pumpkin pie, nor Prudence and Lucille, who were polishing the silver, looked up from their tasks, which struck Meredith as odd.

'Surely not word of a court date already?' she muttered, thinking it was wonderful how efficient the same system that could be so indifferent to the plight of the homeless suddenly ran so smoothly when it came to hounding an old lady over a few dollars' worth of cheap merchandise.

Squaring her shoulders, she marched down the hall and swung open the door to the living-room, determined to make short work of whoever it was intruding on their weekend. 'Good afternoon,' she announced coldly. 'I believe you've been waiting to see me?'

Then all her equanimity disintegrated in dizzying waves as her visitor rose up from the chair by the hearth and swung around to face her, his tall figure casting shadows over the lamplit walls.

'Yes,' Tom said, 'for far too long. How are you, Meredith?'

Too nonplussed to care that she sounded ungracious and hostile, she said the first words that came into her head. 'Why are *you* here?'

For a moment, his wonderful blue eyes clouded. If she hadn't known him to be the most self-assured man ever created, she'd have thought him uncertain of his welcome. He took a step towards her. 'To help,' he said. 'What else?'

She had dreamed of this moment so often, had tried to imagine how she would feel—the lilting excitement, the rush of love, the joy, the optimism. She'd imagined him coming to the door, his arms full of roses, a ring in his pocket, his heart on his sleeve. She'd pictured him sweeping her into his arms, erasing all the hurt with his kisses, his words. Silly, adolescent clichés, perhaps, but she'd nurtured them for months. Yet it took only seconds for his reply to shatter all her illusions. The meeting fell so far short of her hopes that it induced in her nothing but a cold, sick disappointment. 'Why would we need your help?' she asked dully. 'The roof isn't leaking.'

'I heard about Eleanor,' he said.

Suddenly, she understood the giddy excitement of last night, the veiled looks, her feeling that something devious was under way. They had called and asked him to help, told him what had happened to Eleanor. And what else? That she herself was desolate without him, that she looked pale and thin and had walked the floors for nights after he'd first left?

'Go to bed, Meredith. You look like death warmed over…most unattractive. You want to look your best for tomorrow,' Lucille had said. And Dolores, reading the leaves: 'flowers, rice, organ music.' Dear heaven, they were already planning the wedding! What sort of bribe had they offered him to get him out here so quickly? And what did the next phase of their plan involve?

Embarrassment consumed her. 'How very kind, but you shouldn't have put yourself to so much trouble. I can manage very well without you.'

She stood with her back to the light so that her face was in shadow and he wouldn't be able to see how greedily her eyes devoured him. He was wearing a hand-knit sweater and expertly tailored trousers that emphasised the length of his legs, and she noticed an expensive leather jacket slung over the arm of one of the chairs. His face was still dark from the sun, even though her own tan had long since faded.

'What if I can't manage very well without you?' he asked softly, and moved to close the gap that separated them.

He would have touched her if she'd let him. Stepping quickly past him, she put a safe distance between them. He didn't have to know how she was shaking inside, how terribly afraid she was that he might try to break her heart again, and this time succeed. 'Don't be ridiculous, Tom,' she said. 'What can a naïve little fool like me offer a big sophisticated man like you?'

His brows drew together in a scowl. 'Will you please stop all this, Meredith?'

'Stop what?' His aftershave reached out to tease her senses, evoking memories so potent that she could have wept. She could hardly endure having him so close and not run her fingertips along his smoothly shaven jaw.

'This meaningless chit-chat. We're not exactly strangers thrown together by chance, with nothing to discuss but the weather.'

'Really? Then exactly what are we? Friends?' She looked him full in the eye and uttered an empty little laugh. 'I hardly think so. Friends don't run out on each other. Lovers?' Another laugh, this one so scornful she hardly recognised it as hers. 'Scarcely. The word implies some sort of mutual affection.'

'Meredith——'

'I've got it—a one-night stand!'

'That's enough!'

'For you, perhaps,' she taunted, wilfully misunderstanding him, enjoying baiting him. 'No doubt that's the sort of liaison you prefer, but I don't want——'

'Stop it!' he roared, his temper erupting so suddenly that she faltered, afraid she'd pushed him too far. 'Damn it, Meredith, stop all this insane babbling and give me a chance to talk, to explain!'

'You had a chance,' she yelled back, mortified at the sudden tears that clustered along her lashes. She'd thought herself past the crying stage weeks ago. 'Back in the summer, when I stood in front of half the town and made a fool of myself over you! It's too late now for explanations. What you've got to say doesn't matter any more.'

'Oh, it matters,' he muttered, his eyes shooting sparks, and before she could evade it his arm snaked out and caught her to him so suddenly that the breath was knocked out of her. And then, as quickly as it had arisen, his temper fled, chased away by some other emotion that softened the hard line of his mouth and left him looking lost and unhappy.

'Don't,' she whispered, trying to push him away with hands that longed to wind around his neck and hold him close.

Given half a chance, he would steal her heart all over again, and her soul, his mouth cajoling her with well-remembered kisses and softly murmured words that suggested happy-ever-after without promising her anything. And she was close to letting him get away with it. Again.

'No!' With her last remaining handful of resistance, she shoved away from him before it was too late.

Surprised, he released her, allowed her to slip from his embrace. 'Meredith, sweetheart...?'

He looked so bewildered, so bereft, that she had to harden her heart. It wasn't fair that she was so susceptible to his every nuance of emotion.

'Let's not pretend this is why you came back,' she said, before the bruised and puzzled expression in his vivid eyes undid her. 'You say you're here for Eleanor, and if that's true then I have no right to ask you to leave, because she does need help from someone, and *she* trusts you.'

He didn't miss the implication. 'But I have yet to prove myself with you,' he finished, and shrugged slightly. 'OK—but if you think I'm leaving here again without settling things between you and me, sweet Meredith, then prepare to be wrong.'

She wanted to believe him and dared not. He was back, and the chemistry that she'd never been able to deny was back, too, surging between them more strongly than ever. Even with half a room separating them and him with his hands now safely hooked in the back pockets of his trousers, she could feel him touching her, turning her weak and liquid with need. Fear that he'd destroy her if she didn't remain strong was all that kept her upright.

A wary cough at the door saved her. 'Dinner will be ready in about ten minutes,' Henry said, 'so I thought an aperitif might be in order. I brought you some sherry.'

'Stay and have some with us,' Meredith begged.

'No, no.' Too discreet for his own good, Henry placed a tray on the coffee-table. 'I brought only two glasses.'

'I'll get another,' Meredith said, and bolted out of the room before either of the men could object.

Except for Prudence and Eleanor, everyone else was clustered in the hall, excitement and curiosity written all over their faces. 'Well?' Florence whispered impatiently.

'We had to send Henry in to find out what was happening,' Dolores apologised. 'We were . . . well, worried—because everything got so quiet all of a sudden.'

'Nosy's the word you're looking for,' Bill said with relish. 'You'd have been peeping through the keyhole in another minute.'

'But we hadn't meant for Henry to stay and sip sherry with Thomas,' Lucille was indignant. 'Get back in there at once, Meredith and send that old fool back out.'

Meredith shook both fists at them. 'You did this!' she hissed. 'You went behind my back and brought him here. How could you?'

'We did not. He came of his own accord,' Florence insisted.

'Then how did he know about Eleanor?'

'I told him.'

'Exactly!'

'When he phoned.'

'He wouldn't have known unless you'd—*he phoned*?' Shock made Meredith forget to whisper and sent her voice shooting up half an octave. Stunned, she looked at the faces around her, found confirmation in their smiles. Even Bill looked pleased. *'Tom phoned here?'*

'Yesterday, right after Abel Myers left,' Florence told her.

'What did he want?'

'Oh, this and that.' Florence fiddled with her apron strings and tried to look vague. 'Asked how everyone was, of course, so naturally I told him what had happened.'

'You should have let me know, Florence.'

'Well, I was going to, but he said not to bother mentioning it, that he'd be on the first flight out this morning and take care of things in person.'

'What else did you tell him, besides the news about Eleanor?'

'I just answered questions. We only talked for about ten minutes.'

Answered questions for ten minutes? Meredith shuddered. Florence wasn't one to waste words. She could give a succinct account of a person's entire life in half the time.

'But you might as well know I insisted he stay the entire Thanksgiving weekend, since he had no other plans. Lord knows when he last enjoyed a home-cooked meal.'

Meredith slumped against the wall. 'Lord knows,' she agreed faintly.

'You seem less than delighted, Meredith,' Lucille observed caustically. 'We had expected a little more gratitude.'

'I just wish someone had consulted me first, Lucille. I happen to feel we'd be better off hiring someone more . . . impersonally connected.' Someone who didn't have compelling blue eyes and laugh-lines; someone without charm or looks or anything else to recommend him except brains. In short, anyone who didn't remind her of starry nights scented with summer, or the terrible emptiness of lost love.

'Put aside your own feelings, child, until Eleanor's problems have been resolved. You might as well accept that you're going to have to live under the same roof with Thomas, at least for the next few days.' Lucille smiled archly, a scheming old matchmaker if ever Meredith saw one. 'If, after that, you still want to see the back of him, I dare say he'll go with good grace.'

'Don't count on it, Lucille,' Tom said from the doorway of the living-room, his voice so loaded with gentle menace that Meredith broke out in goose-bumps. 'I'm not leaving until I've accomplished everything I came for.'

CHAPTER NINE

'AND that's all you've been able to find out?' Tom chewed the end of his pen consideringly.

'We can't get her to tell us anything, except that she didn't do it,' Dolores said. 'We hoped, when we told her you were here, that she'd brighten up a bit, but she's . . . I don't know exactly, but it's as if she's afraid of something.'

'Or someone.' Tom nodded absently as Florence offered him more coffee. Dinner was over but, instead of gathering in the living-room as usual, they'd all remained seated at the big round table, filling in as many details as possible on Eleanor's misfortune while Tom took notes and asked questions. 'I'll get a copy of the official police report first thing tomorrow,' he said at last, 'and I plan to have a little chat with the personnel at Ryan's when the store opens on Tuesday, but it's what Eleanor has to say that I'm most interested in hearing.'

'That'll have to wait until morning,' Meredith insisted curtly. 'She's already settled for the night and if you disturb her now and bring all this up again, she won't sleep.'

'Of course.' He turned reproachful eyes on her, managing to instill her full of guilt for having assumed he'd disagree. 'I'm here to help, not make things worse, Meredith. I have no intention of routing her out of bed or giving her the third degree.

I agree with what you said earlier. There's something strange about this whole situation and I aim to get to the bottom of it—but not at the expense of Eleanor's health. She needs protection and proper representation, and, whether you like it or not, I'm the best qualified person to see that she gets them.'

Meredith went to bed hoping he was right and that he'd have everything sorted out and be on his way by the end of the long weekend. Just being in the same room with him was making treacherous inroads into her hard-won peace of mind. Seeing him, hearing his voice, watching his hands smooth the sheet of paper in front of him, his mouth close softly over the end of his pen—all stirred up erotic parallels that even now, three months later, had the power to leave her weak.

As for that near-kiss this afternoon, all it had done was confirm that memory had not played her false. In his embrace, she became complete, all the parts of her that no one else had ever reached flowing together to create a whole woman. Once a person had experienced that, having to settle for anything less was like looking through an out-of-focus telescope. All the sharp, exciting clarity of awareness became blunted. Meredith had somehow learned to cope with such impairment the first time he'd robbed her of it, but she doubted she could do so twice.

After breakfast the next morning, while Tom walked down to the police station to see what he could discover, Meredith tried to persuade Eleanor to come downstairs. But despair or fear, or whatever it was that had gripped her the day before, had tightened its hold, taking Eleanor further into a world removed from the people and events around her. She would not be lured downstairs.

'Then I'll have to go and talk to her up there,' Tom declared on his return, when Meredith explained.

'She's very fragile,' Meredith warned him. 'She's in no shape to deal with any of this.'

'Well, someone has to,' he retorted flatly. 'According to this report, it's a cut-and-dried case. She was seen putting things in her bag, caught leaving the store without paying for them, and neither denied the charges nor offered any explanations for her behaviour.'

'Preposterous!' Lucille snorted. 'I'd like to hear what this Myers child has to say about everything. It strikes me his story's a little too pat to be convincing.'

A wicked smile inched over Tom's mouth. 'I'm way ahead of you, Lucille,' he told her, heading for the stairs.

'Now just hold on a minute!' Meredith objected, hurrying after him but, as always, his legs covered ground twice as fast as hers, and before she could catch up with him he was in the upper hall.

'Eleanor, make yourself decent! I'm coming in,' he bellowed, flinging open one door after another, looking for her.

'She's in here,' Meredith snapped, indicating the old master bedroom overlooking the park, 'and there's no need to yell. She's not that hard of hearing, and you'll just upset her even more.'

'Sometimes yelling is the only thing that gets results,' Tom said, striding through the doorway. 'That and a lot of bluff.'

Eleanor sat huddled in a chair by the window, looking transparent enough for a sudden gust of wind to blow her away. She didn't acknowledge either of them by so much as a glance and Meredith's heart missed a beat. It wouldn't take much more to push Eleanor into a serious decline.

Tom crossed the room and squatted in front of her. 'I've come a long way to see you, Eleanor,' he said gently, taking her hands and squeezing them. 'Aren't you at least going to say hello?'

She stirred a little, her eyes flickering towards him then away again.

It's not going to work, Meredith thought despondently, realising for the first time how much she'd been counting on Tom's presence to effect a miracle, at least where Eleanor was concerned.

He, however, was less easily discouraged. 'I've missed you very much, Eleanor,' he said with such sincerity that Meredith's eyes prickled with tears. What she wouldn't give to receive such heartfelt reassurance from him; to know beyond question that his strength and loyalty were there for her to call on whenever she needed them.

For the longest time, Eleanor remained still, then, just when Meredith was ready to lose hope that anyone could reach her, she spoke, her voice like the rustle of dead leaves after a long, cold winter. 'I missed you all the time, Tommy. I never forgot you.'

'Then let me help you now.'

She turned puzzled eyes on him. 'Why?'

'Because I want everyone to know what a good person you are.' Without releasing her hands, he rose to his feet and sat on the wide window-sill next to her. 'What happened in Ryan's store, Eleanor?'

'I don't know.'

For a second or two, Tom didn't speak. Then, to Meredith's horror, he said, 'You stole things. You put things in your bag without paying for them.'

'He isn't telling the truth,' Eleanor said in a broken whisper.

'Who isn't?' Tom was instantly alert, a legal bloodhound on the scent.

'That boy...the one who...' She lapsed into silence, clearly afraid to continue.

'What? Tell me, Eleanor.'

'I was only looking,' she began hesitantly, but it was as though, once she allowed the door in her mind to open a crack, everything she'd kept locked in there came spilling out. 'It was so cold in the park and I hadn't looked in the shops for such a long time.'

'Did you see anything you liked?' Tom asked.

'Some soap...lavender, it was. I could smell it through the wrapping, but there was such a crowd in there and such a long line up at the counter—lots of young people, you know, buying records and make-up—and the music was so loud that it made my head hurt. So I just left the soap on top of some books. I know I should have put it back where it belonged. Lucille says I'm always leaving things lying around for other people to fall over, but I was so tired, Tommy.'

'I understand,' he said. 'Some days I come home from work so bushed, I just drop my clothes on the bedroom floor and leave them until Freda picks them up.'

Who's Freda? Meredith wondered, stabbed with such sudden painful jealousy that she had to turn away in case he saw it reflected in her expression.

'Is she your wife, Tommy?'

He laughed. 'Not likely! What woman would want a slob like me for a husband?'

Meredith busied herself tidying the bedspread and squashed the wimpy little inner voice that wanted to shout, I would!

'No,' he continued, 'Freda's my cleaning lady who comes in once a week. What happened after you left the soap on top of the books, Eleanor?'

'I was going to come home when the men started checking people's shopping bags. And suddenly, that bad boy and his friends were next to me, and he reached into my bag——'

'What bag? You said you hadn't bought anything.'

'No, but I always take my straw bag when I go out. I don't feel right without it.'

Meredith nodded at Tom's enquiring glance. No matter if all she planned was a stroll to the nearest park bench, Eleanor never ventured forth without her big bag.

His gaze swung back to Eleanor. 'Did Steven Myers take something out of your bag?' he asked.

'Oh, no! He took things out of his pockets and put them *in* my bag. And when I tried to get away from him, his friends stood in my way, and he held my arm so tight that it hurt. I've got bruises, here above my elbow.' She pushed back the loose sleeve

of her dressing-gown and showed him two purple
spots on her milk-pale skin.

Meredith's rage wouldn't be contained. 'Eleanor,
why didn't you tell us all this before?'

'She's telling us now,' Tom said conversa-
tionally, and if Meredith hadn't noticed the little
white lines that all at once bracketed his mouth,
she'd have thought him quite unmoved. 'Did he say
anything, Eleanor?'

Her voice trembled. 'Yes, Tommy.'

Leaning down, he traced the outline of her
bruises with a very gentle finger. 'Tell us what he
said, sweetheart.'

Meredith's heart clutched in brief agony. Heaven
help her, she still loved this man, not just because
he'd taught her the real meaning of passion, but
because he was good and decent and kind.

Eleanor's eyes swam with tears again. 'He said
that if I told anyone, anyone at all, Tommy, that
I knew what would happen.'

'And what is that?' Idly, he stroked his thumbs
over the backs of her hands.

'That no one would believe me because they never
do. Everyone knows I forget things and I get mixed
up. I'm senile, you know.'

Meredith felt as if an iron fist had slammed her
hard in the midriff. 'Eleanor!' she gasped. 'Who
ever told you such a cruel, wicked lie?'

'That boy told me.'

'But why would you listen to him? You hardly
know him.'

'I see him sometimes.'

'Where?'

'Here.'

Meredith exchanged puzzled glances with Tom and shook her head at the question she read in his eyes. To her knowledge, Steven Myers had never visited the house.

'Tell us about that,' Tom invited casually. 'When was he last here?'

Eleanor looked vague. 'I don't remember. He comes when everyone else has gone to bed.'

'And what does he want?'

'Henry's wine,' Eleanor said without hesitation. 'He sneaks in through that window to the cellar, the one under the front porch.'

'I see.' Releasing her hands, Tom stood up. 'And he knows you saw him doing that, does he?'

She nodded.

'Why didn't you tell Meredith or Henry? Why did you let him go on frightening you like that?'

'Because he said...' restlessly, Eleanor clutched her dressing-gown around her and drifted over to perch next to Meredith on the bed '... he said that no one would believe me. I didn't know his name then, you see, and he said people would just think I was making up stories so that I wouldn't get blamed for stealing. And then Meredith would have to send me away. He said I'd be a bag lady again, Tommy.'

Meredith reached over and wrapped her arms around Eleanor. 'No, darling!' she said fiercely. 'Not as long as I have breath left in my body. This is your home and no one will ever send you away.'

'We're going to get one of the others to help you dress now,' Tom said, staring down at the garden, his back to them. 'Meredith and I are going to sort out this whole mess, and you're not to worry any more, you hear? When we get back, I want to see you downstairs, wearing your best dress and with your hair brushed, ready for Thanksgiving dinner. Do we have a deal?'

'Oh, Tommy!' Eleanor's tremulous laugh held the ghost of a young girl's giggle. 'You always say that when you want to get around me, because you know I always say "yes".'

They walked through the park to the Myers' house. The sky was overcast and a chill wind blew off the river, the forerunner of winter's bitter cold. It didn't seem to bother Tom that the silence between them was full of seething tension, but Meredith's nerves were stretched tight.

'Quite a change since you were here in the summer,' she said, indicating the brilliant foliage on the trees. 'It's turned very cold in the last couple of weeks.'

'I don't want to talk about the weather, Meredith,' he said, not bothering to look her way.

'Do you want to talk about Eleanor?'

'No.'

Rebuffed, she hurried to keep pace with him. Ahead, two squirrels bounded through fallen leaves, eyes bright and inquisitive, fur gleaming. She tried again. 'I'm sorry I wasn't more welcoming yesterday.'

'Let's not start exchanging apologies. I don't have that much time to spare right now. There are more important tasks to accomplish.'

'Well, at least let me say that I'm glad you're here. For Eleanor, that is. You're the only person able to get through to her in all this. You were very kind with her, and very gentle, and she really believes in you.'

'I don't want your gratitude, either. Stop trying to make me out to be better than I am. My original reasons for coming back were purely selfish and had nothing to do with Eleanor.'

He had zipped up his leather jacket against the wind, and stuffed his hands in his pockets. The cold, or perhaps the anger that she sensed had been simmering in him since before they left the house, intensified the brilliance of his eyes and emphasised the lean severity of his jaw.

'What were your original reasons?' Meredith asked in a tiny voice as they approached the gates on the far side of the park. It was insane, no doubt, but a spark of hope flickered in her heart that perhaps their final chapter had not after all been written.

He swung an oblique glance her way. 'All in good time, Meredith. This is not the place to go into them. Quite apart from anything else, we are not alone.'

On the path ahead, Cal Gibson sauntered towards them, his dog at his heels. Meredith braced herself. She hadn't forgotten the last time Cal had seen her with Tom.

'You can pretend you're not with me, if you like,' Tom murmured.

'I'm not the one who runs away from confrontations,' she reminded him sharply, and forced herself to smile at Cal. 'Good morning!'

'Morning, Meredith.' Cal slowed and nodded civilly at Tom. 'Heard you were back. More problems with the house?'

'In a manner of speaking,' Tom replied, and bent to scratch the retriever's ears. The dog shimmied with pleasure, her plumed tail swishing back and forth, and butted her head against him, begging for more. 'Nice dog.'

Was there a female alive able to resist him? Meredith wondered.

'Didn't know you liked dogs, you being such a city type.' Cal sounded as surprised as if the devil himself had sprung a halo. 'Never had one when you lived here as a boy, did you?'

'I tried.'

A sudden grin cracked the weathered features of Cal's face. 'You mean the time you stole that watchdog from the lumber yard?'

'I didn't steal it,' Tom protested. 'It followed me home.'

'After you climbed over the fence and opened the gate from the inside.' Cal allowed himself a rusty chuckle. 'You were hell on wheels as a kid, Tom Whitney, but you livened things up, I have to admit. How long are you planning to stay this time?'

'As long as it takes,' Tom replied ambiguously, his gaze settling on Meredith's mouth before drifting down to her hips.

'I heard about the old lady.' Cal fished in his pockets for his cigarettes, and, to Meredith's immense relief, seemed entirely unaware of the roses blooming in her cheeks at Tom's deliberate stare. 'Don't know why Charlie Ryan wants to make an example of her. He's been losing money from shoplifting left, right and centre for weeks, yet he admits she ain't been in the store in months.'

Tom refused the offer of a cigarette and narrowed his eyes. 'What about this so-called witness, Steven Myers? What sort of a kid is he?'

'I play poker with his grandaddy who thinks the sun rises and sets on the boy, so if you quote me on this I'll deny having said it.' Cal squinted against the smoke blowing in his eyes from his cigarette. 'But in my opinion that kid's a nasty piece of work, and I'd sooner believe my Honey here is a cat in disguise as pay mind to anything Steven Myers swears to be the truth.'

Hearing mention of her name, the dog thumped her tail. Tom fondled her ears again. 'I'll bear your opinion—and your wishes—in mind.'

Cal nodded and prepared to move on. 'Well, good luck to you. I'm glad the old lady's got you on her side.' Another grin split his face. 'I reckon, if anyone's a match for Steven Myers, it's you.'

'Gee, thanks—I think!' Tom said wryly.

'Don't get me wrong.' Cal stopped and turned to face them again. 'I ain't saying you're alike. You were a lot of things when you were a kid, but you were never a liar.' Again that rusty chuckle. 'Might have been better off if you had been. Part of the trouble folks had with you was your mouth! But Steven Myers...he's another story. Lies so much, he doesn't know he's doing it, and thinks everyone else is too stupid to know, either. It's about time he found out differently.' He nodded again. 'Be seeing you around, no doubt. Happy Thanksgiving.'

Meredith blinked as Cal went on his way, and turned to Tom in delight. 'He was almost friendly!' she exclaimed.

For a moment, she thought he was going to reach out and touch her, but at the last minute he changed his mind and started walking briskly towards the park exit. 'Does it matter all that much to you how the people around here feel?' he asked, looking thoughtful. 'Are they that important to you?'

'Yes,' she replied without hesitation. 'In a town this size, it matters.'

His blue eyes scanned the street. Mature maples, planted around the turn of the century, lined both boulevards, their branches curving to form a tunnel of shade during the summer. Behind tall hedges, well-kept older homes sat in neat and spacious gardens. Such properties would be worth a small fortune in Toronto, he thought.

It was the sort of neighbourhood where generations of the same families stayed to raise their children, the sort of place where no youngster would ever find himself turned away from a door if he needed help. If it didn't possess the electric energy of the city, it had a certain charm, a gracious permanence that struck a surprisingly comforting note. A man could find himself again in such a place, maybe even heal wounds so old he'd forgotten how he ever came by them.

'Have you thought of moving away from here—to a city, perhaps, where neighbours are more inclined to mind their own business?' he asked Meredith.

She shook her head, uncertain where the conversation was leading. 'Cities are so impersonal. I need to feel I belong, Tom.'

'Yeah.' He nodded. 'I guess I already knew that, but I had to make sure. Isn't that the Myers' house up ahead?'

'Yes.'

'Then let's get this over with.'

Conducted on the front doorstep, it was not a pleasant interview. Steven Myers was a shifty-eyed fourteen-year-old with a bad case of acne and a mouth Tom itched to shut with the back of his hand. 'You've not got nothin' on me,' the boy muttered, working a wad of gum between his teeth and upper lip, and peering sullenly at them when Tom outlined the reason for their visit. 'You got no right coming here and buggin' me.'

At that moment, Abel Myers, who lived next door, came hurrying through a gap in the hedge. 'What's all this?' he demanded. 'What business have you got, Tom Whitney, barging in uninvited and harassing decent folks in the privacy of their homes on Thanksgiving Sunday?'

'Tell him, Steven,' Tom coaxed with gentle threat. 'Tell him what really happened in Ryan's store.'

'I don't know nothin', Grandad, except what I told you,' Steven whined. 'This guy's just trying to make trouble.'

'Get off my son's property before I haul you in for trespassing,' Abel Myers said.

Tom laughed delightedly. 'Oh, please do! I'm sure the neighbours would get a kick out of it. But make sure you haul in your grandson at the same time, because I intend to press charges against him, and it'll save you having to make two trips.'

'Charges against Stevie? On what grounds?'

'Breaking and entering. Theft. Blackmail. Assault. Perjury—and that's just for openers.'

Chief Myers turned a dark and ugly red. 'You want to watch your tongue, Tom Whitney. It's going to land you in trouble. You can't go around maligning decent citizens in this town and get away with it.'

'But that's not what I'm doing, Chief,' Tom explained gently. 'I'm talking about your grandson, and there's nothing at all decent about him. Is there, Steven?'

'He's nuts,' the boy muttered. 'Get rid of him, Grandad.'

Tom smiled at him. 'How many friends do you have around here, Steven?'

'Plenty.'

'Like those you were with in Ryan's store on Friday? The ones who stood by while you let an old lady take the blame for the stuff you'd stolen? The ones who were only too glad to squeal on you rather than wind up as accessories in a crime that could get them two years' probation and about a hundred hours of community work?'

'They didn't squeal.'

Tom's smile grew broader. 'Like frightened little pigs, kiddo!'

Steven Myers' bravado dwindled abruptly. 'How come you're just picking on me? They took stuff as well. They just didn't get caught, is all.'

'Pretty rough, huh?' Tom oozed sympathy. 'I guess a guy never knows who his real buddies are till something like this happens. I bet they were glad enough to help you drink the booze as well, even though *you* had to take all the risks getting it.'

'They were there, too! They got a charge out of scaring the old woman. And half the stuff that got shoved in her bag on Friday was theirs as well. Geez, wait——'

'What booze?' Abel Myers' face grew even darker. 'Ryan's don't sell booze.'

'I'm sorry, I forgot you didn't know about the break-ins at my house. Do you want to tell him, Stevie, or shall I?'

'Don't say another word, Steven!' the chief of police barked, glaring at his grandson's pasty expression and apparently not liking what it told him. 'Just go inside and leave me to handle this.'

'Grandaddy——'

'This minute, Steven!'

'Well,' Tom said, once the front door had closed behind the boy, 'I suppose you'd like to haul me down to the station now, and we can——'

'You're bluffing, Tom Whitney! You don't have a thing on Steven.'

'Chief Myers, after what the three of us just heard, I've got everything I need on Steven, and you and I both know it.'

'His buddies wouldn't tell you anything. Those kids have stuck by one another since they were in kindergarten together.'

'Then they'll no doubt enjoy sharing the same probation officer.' Tom cupped Meredith's elbow and pointed her in the direction of the front gate. 'Now, shall we go take care of the formalities?'

'Just a minute.'

Already halfway down the path, Tom stopped and looked back at Abel Myers. Meredith could hardly keep her face straight at the choirboy innocence of his expression. 'Have I overlooked something, Chief?' he enquired blandly.

'It's Thanksgiving.'

'Yes.' Tom consulted his watch. 'In fact, we're in rather a hurry to get back in time for our turkey dinner, so if we could speed things up a little...?'

'Yes, well...Steven's at a difficult age.'

'Is that what makes him so rude, or was he born that way?'

Abel Myers glowered. 'I suppose it's asking too much for someone like you to show a bit of understanding. I suppose, because we've had our differences in the past, that you'd get a vengeful sort of pleasure out of turning the boy over to the juvenile authorities.'

'Not at all. I happen to remember very well what it's like to be a kid with no one willing to go to bat for me, and it's not something I'd wish on any youngster. On the other hand, I'm not going to let him victimise innocent bystanders.'

'If I were to deal with him...?'

'Am I to understand,' Tom enquired smoothly, 'that you're admitting I have just cause to pursue the matter if I choose? That Steven gave false evidence and incriminated a harmless old lady in order to save his own skin?'

'If I were to talk to Charlie Ryan, explain there'd been a misunderstanding, get him to drop the charges, would you let me deal privately with my grandson?'

Tom shook his head in disgust. 'You know better than that, Chief. I want a public apology from the store. Front-page coverage in the *Times*.'

'And if you get it?'

'We have a deal.' Another smile, loaded with charming threat, slid over Tom's face. 'I'm sure you'll impress on the boy how unpleasant the consequences will be if he ever sets foot on my property again, or harasses any members of my household.'

'Lord,' the police chief fumed, 'you're enjoying this, aren't you? You've been waiting years for a chance to get back at me.'

'I want to see that apology in Wednesday's edition, Chief Myers, or I'll be paying you another visit—a more official visit that won't be so easily kept private,' Tom said coldly and turned away, propelling Meredith ahead of him down the path to the road.

'You were wonderful!' she gasped, half running to keep up with him as they re-entered the park. 'I didn't know you'd checked out the boy's friends and had all that evidence.'

'I hadn't.'

She wrenched her arm free and ran ahead to face him. 'You mean you were bluffing? All that stuff about knowing he'd broken into the house and stolen the wine?'

'Every last word,' Tom agreed solemnly.

Meredith started to giggle. 'That isn't legal.'

'Not in the least. I'd have a hard time making charges stick. The courts don't condone entrapment.' He grinned down at her. 'However, when the situation calls for it, I'll play as dirty as I have to.'

He was backing her over the grass and towards the trees, she realised. Hanging on to his arms to keep herself from tripping, she asked, 'Do you resort to playing dirty often?'

He closed in on her, his hands tugging her towards him until her body was curved against his in sweet compliance. 'Only when I absolutely have to,' he rumbled against her mouth. 'You know that old saying: "all's fair in love and war".'

'And was that war?' she asked dreamily, mesmerised by his fingers threading through her curls and imprisoning her so that she was drowning in the endless depths of his eyes.

'Indeed,' he whispered with delicious, silky menace. 'And now I'm free to get on with what I really came back for. And I'm prepared to fight dirty on that, too.'

Then he brought his lips slanting down across hers so persuasively that, insane or not, she could resist him no longer. Regardless of the chilly wind weaving its way inside her jacket or the leaves drifting against her ankles, she kissed him back with a hunger she couldn't begin to disguise.

CHAPTER TEN

THEY walked home openly holding hands like young lovers, and, although linked fingers were hardly symptomatic of a future together, Meredith found herself dangerously tempted to hope again. He hadn't really said anything specific, but something about him had changed.

Perhaps it had been there for her to see from the minute she'd found him in the living-room the day before, and she'd been too busy throwing up defences to recognise it. Perhaps his lawyer's mind had wanted to settle all other matters before resolving the most delicate issue between them, and that was why he'd deliberately held back until now. Or perhaps it had something to do with what had happened in the last hour or so. Maybe Cal's tacit approval had been the catalyst, or even Abel Myers' reluctant concessions. All she knew was that the tension in Tom was gone.

For once, he was content to stroll, to take the time to look around and enjoy autumn's brilliant display; to settle his glance on her and let it linger there, the hint of a smile and a promise in his eyes. It was as though he'd stopped running, as though he'd arrived at some personal milestone.

They took the long way back to the house, coming up the main drive to the front entrance. 'We're home,' he said—a strange choice of words for him—and, grasping her about the waist in his big strong hands, he swung her up the steps to the veranda.

There was no one to greet them, and while Tom hung their jackets in the closet Meredith peeped into the dining-room. The family had been busy. The table was already set with Lucille's best lace cloth and good china. The whole house smelled heavenly, the aroma of sage and thyme mingling with the sharp scent of chrysanthemums and a faint tang of smoke from the apple wood burning in the fireplaces.

'Where is everybody?' Tom wondered aloud. 'I thought they'd be lined up at the window, waiting for us to get back.'

Lucille's voice floated down to them from the upper landing. 'That would intimate we had reason to worry, and it simply never occurred to me that we had cause.'

She came down the stairs, regal in ancient black velvet, blue-rinsed hair immaculate, pearls that might have been real around her throat. Siamantha stepped daintily in her tracks and complained softly at being ignored.

Dolores, her dark eyes snapping with excitement, popped her head around the kitchen door. 'I thought I heard voices. They're back, everybody!'

'What happened?' Behind Dolores, Florence came out into the hall, hands encased in oven mitts, followed by Prudence and Henry.

'Plenty,' Lucille smirked, bending to sweep Siamantha into her arms. 'They were holding hands all the way up the drive.'

'I thought you weren't watching,' Bill grumbled from the living-room.

Lucille raised aristocratic brows. 'Eavesdropping, William?'

'Trying to nap in front of the fire, which is damn near impossible with you nattering away all the time,' he replied testily, and came forward to fix Tom in a severe gaze. 'Well, boy, don't just stand there looking moonstruck. Did you manage to clear Eleanor, or what?'

'I believe Eleanor deserves to be the first to hear the details on that,' Tom said, and grinned at Henry and Prudence who stood clutching two bottles of wine apiece. 'However, I think it's safe to say you can open those and start celebrating. Now, where is Eleanor?'

'Resting in her room,' Prudence said. 'She's all dressed and I helped her put her hair up, but she wanted to sit quietly by herself and look through her box of mementoes. She likes to do that once in a while when she feels a bit out of sorts. It seems to comfort her.'

'They aren't her mementoes,' Lucille declared. 'They're items she's helped herself to out of the attic. Poor old thing, I suppose it's because, unlike me, she never had anything of her own to begin with.'

'She has her respectability,' Tom pointed out, 'which is more than a lot of people can claim. Come on, Meredith, let's go and tell her what happened.'

Eleanor sat by her window, a baby's christening gown spread across her lap. She stroked the fine yellowed silk, her eyes fixed on him devotedly as Tom told her she was cleared of guilt and her reputation restored.

'So there you have it, Eleanor,' he concluded, and was half stooped to kiss her lightly rouged cheek when he noticed a silver-framed snapshot on the table beside her.

Straightening, he picked it up and examined it. 'I remember this!' he exclaimed in a wondering, far-away sort of voice. 'I remember this rocking-horse.'

'Logan McDonald, who used to own the hardware shop, made it especially for you,' Eleanor said calmly.

'It had a long woolly tail.'

Eleanor nodded. 'And a red mane to match.'

'A sudden stillness crept over Tom. 'How did you know that? This isn't a colour print.'

Leaning closer, Meredith peered at the photograph. It showed a little boy astride a wooden horse, and a woman holding him in place and directing his attention towards the camera. Behind them, a veranda stood half shaded by a lilac tree in full bloom. The background was a little out of focus, but not enough to disguise the Whitney property in its prime.

'Eleanor,' Tom asked again, and Meredith noticed that his hand was trembling, 'how did you know the tail and mane were red?'

'Because I gave you the horse on your second birthday, Tommy, and Victor took this picture of us.'

'Victor? Victor who?'

'Why, Victor Kennedy, of course! I married him later that year and we went to live in California.'

Tom's fingers, so strong as a carpenter's, so gentle as a lover's, fumbled clumsily as he tried to pry loose the back of the frame. Meredith took it from him, slid free the snapshot and placed it in his hands.

Turning it over, he studied the inscription on the back. 'Nellie with Tommy, May 6th, 1956. Riverbridge, B.C.,' he read, and sat down rather abruptly on the bed. 'Good lord!' His voice choked in his throat.

How had they managed to miss the obvious? Meredith wondered, her own eyes misting at the expression she detected in his. That intense, often Arctic blue had softened as though it had been touched by a more temperate sun.

Suddenly all Eleanor's apparent eccentricities made perfect, logical sense. Her unflagging trust in a man who was a stranger and a threat to the rest of them, her devastation when he left, her faith in his innate goodness, even her use of the childish 'Tommy' when everyone else called him 'Tom'— why hadn't they questioned it all sooner, and made the connection?

Eleanor picked up the gown in her lap. 'This was your christening robe. I made it by hand for you, right after you were born. Oh, Tommy,' she said dreamily, 'you were such a beautiful baby, such thick dark hair, such big eyes.'

She laughed, the ghost of that much younger woman emerging more strongly. 'And *so* naughty! You were walking at nine months, and after that no one could keep up with you. But how I loved you, and how I missed you when I went away.'

'Aunt Nellie?' Tom tried out the words, rolling them around in his mouth like a man learning a foreign language.

'I knew you'd remember, because I prayed so hard that you would! It's true that if you wish for something badly enough, you'll get it in the end.' Eleanor laughed again delightedly, but Tom's eyes were glazed with tears and Meredith suddenly felt superfluous, an intruder on a moment that belonged only to Tom and his aunt. She had a thousand questions, but they'd have to wait. This was not her reunion to share. Quietly, she let herself out of the room.

Much later, after she'd soaked in the bath and changed into a rose-pink challis dress with a softly flared skirt and batwing sleeves, she went looking for him.

'He's upstairs,' Dolores told her. 'Eleanor's in the kitchen having a cup of tea with Prudence, but I think Tom wanted to look through that box of hers for some reason.'

He wasn't in any of the bedrooms, and Meredith finally ran him to earth in the attic. He sat on a trunk, another open and spilling its contents around his feet. She hovered in the doorway, uncertain of her welcome, but he sensed her presence and looked up. 'Hi,' he said, his voice subdued. 'Where'd you get to? I missed you.'

'I thought you'd like to be alone for a while.'

'Not really.' He shrugged helplessly and confessed, 'I feel like such a jerk. How could I not have recognised her? The signs were all there if I'd chosen to see them, and if I needed proof...' He indicated the things he'd found: faded photographs, old birthday cards, a huge leather-bound family Bible.

'You were a baby when she left, Tom. There was no reason to suspect——'

'She came back here after she was widowed, a lonely old lady looking for her roots.' He grabbed blindly for Meredith's hand. 'This Victor she married was a vagabond poet and a lousy provider from all accounts. When he died, she had nothing, no one, so she made her way back to the only real home she'd ever known and found it abandoned. As far as the rest of the world was concerned, she was a homeless old bag lady, and when her one living relative finally showed up he didn't even recognise her.' His shoulders slumped. 'The things we sometimes do, Meredith! How do we learn to forgive ourselves?'

Meredith had never seen him so despondent. 'I think,' she ventured, 'that she's been happy the last few years, Tom.'

He looked up and reached for her other hand, too. 'Oh, honey!' he said, pulling her down beside him on the trunk. 'Don't misunderstand what I'm saying. I'm not criticising you. You probably saved her life, and she thinks the world of you. It's me— my unawareness, the way I trample all over the people I care about the most...'

'You never trampled on Eleanor.' Meredith smiled into his troubled blue eyes. 'And even if you didn't recognise her right away, I know she's forgiven you.'

He framed her face between his hands. 'And what about you, Meredith? Can you forgive me for what I've done to you?'

Her heart thudded wildly. What was he really asking? 'You made it clear how things stood between us from the very start,' she said.

'Did I?' he murmured, his gaze examining her face minutely, lingering on each separate feature as though he'd come close to forgetting what she looked like. 'How odd, since I don't think even I myself knew that. May I kiss you?'

A hiccup of nervous laughter escaped her. 'When did you ever before ask permission?'

'I didn't.' His thumbs traced a path down her throat, delicate as butterflies.

'Then why start now?'

'Because it's no longer a question of my always taking and never giving. I'm not playing fast and loose any more, Meredith. I've changed the rules.'

'You make it sound like a game,' she whispered, her breath catching as his mouth inched closer. 'I thought we'd agreed ... not to play games ...'

'We aren't,' he murmured. 'This is for keeps. Do you mind?'

She tried to shake her head but he immobilised it so that his mouth could find hers. At first he kissed her almost tentatively, seeking her compliance, and then, when she didn't pull away, with an urgency that went beyond mere passion. Their lips clung and shifted, seeking answers to all manner of unspoken questions.

'I've dreamed of you so often,' he whispered against her mouth, his fingers skimming over her from shoulder to hip, confirming the delicate substance of her.

That he might have missed her as badly as she'd missed him was not something she'd ever considered. Last summer, he'd seemed so certain of what he'd wanted, and not once had it included her.

'So many times these last months,' he rushed on, as though to purge himself of all his omissions, 'I've woken in the night aching to reach out and touch you, to hold you next to my heart like this. And then, the next morning, I'd tell myself I was a fool, that I'd chased other dreams too long to forfeit them for something I'd always thought didn't really exist.'

Was that his real reason for returning, to lay to rest, once and for all, the unwelcome ghosts of summer? And was he now feeling differently because of his discovery that Eleanor was his aunt? Meredith wanted to believe he was sincere, but part of her held back. How did she know that his present mood wasn't influenced by the revelations of the afternoon? How did *he* know?

The last few hours had been emotionally draining for him, had left him, perhaps, with an urge to strengthen ties, to reach out to someone—to her. It would be easy to misinterpret the motivation for those feelings today, for him to awaken to a different reality tomorrow, and if that happened she didn't want to be the one caught in the middle. At the same time, she knew that they'd arrived at a crossroads. If they went in separate directions now, they'd never meet again.

She wished she could weave spells to hold him, but realised he had to be master of his own destiny. He had not asked her to give him her heart, and she had no right to demand his. If there was one thing she had learned, it was that love not given freely wasn't worth having. She didn't want promises that rode on the coat-tails of passing emotion. She wanted declarations that came from certainty, passion and commitment that could withstand discovery in the bright light of day.

He watched her face for a sign, hoping for elation and finding only doubt. He couldn't believe how much that frightened him. Had he waited too long to tell her what he'd known in his heart since June? 'You don't believe me, do you?'

Her parted lips were unbelievably pink. He wanted to kiss them again, wanted to slide his hand around her neck and through the tangle of her curls, and draw her against him. He wanted to watch her eyes grow soft and unfocused while he tasted that full and hungry mouth. Most of all, he wanted to possess her, not in order to seduce her into forgiving his belated recognition of her gift of love, but to renew himself in her sweetness. He was incomplete without her, and didn't know how to tell her that—he, a man so persuasive with words that he could sway opposing counsel with his eloquence.

'I'm saying all the wrong things,' he muttered helplessly, 'because I don't know how to handle the feelings I have for you.'

He wanted to tell her that she was different from the other women he'd known with their shiny red lips that spilled invitation without consequences. He was afraid of this half-awakened creature who'd haunted his thoughts for months. The women he knew were beautiful, sleek, polished. She was...pretty. An old-fashioned word, perhaps, but it fitted. She was pretty and good in every way, from the inside out. He probably didn't deserve her, but he needed her desperately.

Want something badly enough and you'll end up getting it, Eleanor had affirmed with her simple faith. He had lusted after success and shunned personal involvement for so long. Was he now to be punished by having his wishes granted, paltry debts repaid to a man who'd only just discovered that they didn't come close to buying real happiness?

He had a sudden vision of the endless years ahead, barren because she wasn't there to share them. A chilling flash of memory resurrected his father's image: the thin, disappointed mouth, the remote and lonely eyes. All at once, he saw himself cast in the same mould, and knew fear for the second time in as many minutes. He didn't want to end up like that, dessicated and alone.

'Meredith,' he groaned, burying his face in her soft and fragrant hair, 'let me love you... please...please...'

She could withstand his rejection, his charm, even his indifference, but never his pain. Turning, she wrapped her arms around him and drew him down to rest his lips against her breasts. She looked down at the well-shaped head she loved so much, and combed her fingers through his hair. Not quite as neatly barbered as usual, it curled up at the ends, defying her efforts to subdue it.

Bending low, she pressed a kiss to his crown and felt the stress in him melt away, displaced by a different kind of tension, a stealthy current that gathered momentum at the acquiescence he sensed in her. His hands strayed from her waist to shape the curve of her ribs, then slid past her hips to test the willingess of her thighs. Desire leapt from his fingertips to embrace her, too.

The afternoon had slipped into dusk, filling the attic with long, quiet shadows that invited intimacy. An old-fashioned lap robe, a relic perhaps from the time the stables had been converted to house the first Whitney automobile, lay at their feet. It was as if heaven had set the stage and was now directing the action.

The lap robe welcomed them; the shadows deepened. Cloaked in secrecy, it didn't matter that the front of her dress gaped open, nudged aside by Tom's mouth searching out her nipples. Only she heard his soft gasp of pleasure when his hand crept up her leg to discover the naked span of warm thigh where her silk stockings ended. And only he witnessed her electric response to his most intimate caress.

How natural it seemed that she should reach for him, how right that only when they were joined in a duet of passion should she feel whole again. If, tomorrow or next week, he were to decide he could not stay, it would be worth the price for the memories he'd leave behind.

The masculine power he exerted, the hunger so finely leashed with tenderness, the hot and violent detonation of passion—these were a legacy no one could ever take away from her. She knew, as his lips settled at last in a gentle sigh against her eyelids, that she would rather live with the pain of losing him than have gone through the years never knowing him.

'I could lie here with you till morning,' he whispered, stirring reluctantly as dusk slid into night, 'and make love to you again and again, but...'

'But the turkey's waiting, and if we stay here much longer someone'll come looking for us,' she finished lightly, remembering how her attempts to cling to the moment once before had succeeded only in driving him away.

As if on cue, Siamantha's querulous tones filtered up the stairs. 'Spare us!' Tom groaned. 'With Siamantha on the prowl, can Lucille be far behind?'

In one lithe motion, he was on his feet, shielding Meredith from the doorway. Regretfully, she fumbled to rearrange her clothing, part of her wanting to stay trapped in the time warp of recent ecstasy, and part of her acknowledging that, whatever its aftermath, she had to face it sooner or later.

Lucille met them on the lower landing. 'What in the world is so fascinating about that attic?' she began, then changed her mind as her observant old eyes swept over them. 'No, don't bother to tell me,' she decided, with disconcerting perception. 'I don't think I want to know.'

Wondering if she looked as guilty as Lucille made her feel, Meredith shrank. 'I'm just going to freshen up before dinner,' she said, and fled into her bedroom.

The dining-room flickered in the light of tall white candles. At the head of the table, Bill carved the turkey. Home-made cranberry sauce, rich as garnets, glistened in a crystal bowl. Pale, delicate wine from Henry's cellar gleamed in long-stemmed glasses.

'You're probably used to something fancier,' Florence said to Tom, 'but we like to stick with tradition, especially at holiday times.'

'Tradition's not something I know much about, but if this meal's any example of what I've been missing I'm willing to learn,' he replied, savouring the rich food with pleasure.

'You'd better pass up your plate for more turkey,' Bill suggested gruffly. 'The way you're going at it, you must have hollow legs.'

'And then tell us what happened when you visited Chief Myers,' Prudence begged. 'We're dying of curiosity.'

Tom raised surprised brows. 'You mean Eleanor hasn't already told you?'

'Eleanor has been more ga-ga than usual,' Lucille informed him tartly. 'Trying to get a sensible word out of her mouth has been beyond any of us. Babbling's the only term to describe what she's been capable of since she came downstairs from her self-imposed exile.'

'Then you'll be pleased to know that Steven Myers confessed to the double crimes of shoplifting and stealing Henry's wine,' Tom said, trying to keep his amusement in check.

Dolores beamed. 'So Eleanor's in the clear?'

'She's more than that.' Tom smiled at Eleanor, who sat next to him, and covered her hand with his. 'She's also my father's sister and my long-lost aunt and godmother.'

Lucille choked on her wine. 'Eleanor, a Whitney?' she yelped. 'Impossible, Thomas! Where did you conceive such an absurd notion?'

'If names and birth dates recorded in the family Bible aren't enough to convince you, Lucille, perhaps my aunt's marriage certificate is.'

Lucille looked thunderstruck. 'Then why in heaven's name didn't she come out and say something before now, instead of cowering in the corner like an unwanted cat?'

'Would you have believed her if she had?'

'Certainly not, but that doesn't excuse *her* behaviour!' Apparently finding nothing amiss in her logic, Lucille bestowed an annoyed frown on Eleanor. 'Do you realise, Eleanor, what all these latterday disclosures mean? All this——' she gestured around the room '—really *is* your home.'

'But it's yours, too, Lucille,' Eleanor said gently.

Shockingly, Lucille's face crumpled and tears trickled from her eyes. 'No, it isn't,' she wept. 'I just pretend it is. The plain fact of the matter is, I don't have a real home any more, and if I died tomorrow no one would miss me or care that I was gone.'

'Rubbish!' Dolores scoffed, a wicked gleam in her eye. 'I read the leaves earlier.' She paused, then continued in her visionary voice, 'They told me you were slated for a grand funeral . . . lots of flowers, organ music——'

'I'm not ready to die quite yet,' Lucille snapped, dabbing away her tears with a tiny lace handkerchief. 'However, I would like to know just what this revelation means in terms of the future. Thomas can hardly turn his own godmother out into the street when the lease expires, can you, Thomas?'

'Hardly, Lucille.'

She beamed. 'Does that mean, dear boy, that you'll agree to let us *all* stay here indefinitely?'

Regretfully, he shook his head. 'I wish I could say yes, but I can't,' he replied, and looked across at Meredith, his eyes reflecting nothing but the golden flames of the candles that separated her from him. 'In fact, I intend to renege on the agreement I drew up last summer, whereby your lease was extended for another year. I'm afraid you're going to have to move much sooner.'

CHAPTER ELEVEN

'YOU'RE a bloody disgrace to humanity, do you know that?' Bill raged. 'I knew I never should have given you the benefit of the doubt! Well, if you think I'm waiting around to be kicked out like some mangy old dog, think again! I'm off, first thing tomorrow. An old folks' home might not offer everything I've grown used to in the last few years, but at least I won't have to worry about finding myself booted out on the street one day.'

Prudence buried her face in her napkin and sobbed quietly while Henry, looking suddenly old and defeated, tried to comfort her. Lucille and Florence stared at each other in mute dismay, and Dolores pressed a hand to her heart, but none of it really registered with Meredith. It was all she could do to deal with her own feelings of betrayal.

Had she endured his initial rejection, and her long and painful recovery from it, only to find, despite all her efforts to prevent it, that she'd succumbed yet again to his fatal charm? If so, then love truly was blind, because now that she paused long enough to think logically he hadn't offered her a single shred of hard evidence that his attitudes or expectations had really changed since last summer.

All at once, it made sense that, after their visit with Steven Myers, the tension in Tom had dissipated. He'd assuaged his conscience by coming back to rescue Eleanor, had atoned for past sins with his grand gesture, and now felt able to walk away unhaunted. Numbly, Meredith started clearing the table of dirty dishes.

'Before you declare an all-out state of war,' Tom said, completely unruffled by the response his statement had provoked, 'let me add that I own a piece of land on the riverfront where I plan to build an adult residential complex that really meets the needs of older, active members of the community—unlike the make-do set-up you have here, which you must agree is less than ideal.' He paused, before adding significantly, 'Of course, I'm going to need a lot of input at the drawing-board stage from the sort of people who'll be living there.'

How well he could manipulate a situation, Meredith thought. If his aim was to topple resistance and defuse anger, he was succeeding admirably.

'People like us, you mean?' Henry offered, hope smoothing the furrows of anxiety from his brow.

Tom nodded. 'Precisely. I want it to be exactly right.' The grin that had so easily lulled Meredith into forgetting his shortcomings flashed over his face. 'After all, I'll probably end up living there myself eventually.'

Bill's high colour was gradually subsiding. 'Not in my time, I hope! You're too hard on my blood-pressure.'

'Actually,' Tom said, 'I have other plans that I hope will keep me busy for at least the next thirty years, so you're probably safe.'

'Very plausible, I'm sure,' Bill retorted, 'but what guarantee can you offer us that you won't suddenly decide to sell the land to someone else? After all, it wouldn't be the first time you've changed your mind where we're concerned, would it?'

'If two representatives from this house are appointed to the board of directors, will that put your mind at ease? Or if I tell you that I intend to dedicate the place to my aunt and godmother, Eleanor Whitney-Kennedy, will that be enough to convince you?'

'It's a start,' Bill conceded.

Tom pressed home his advantage. 'Naturally, as charter residents, you'd all have first choice of accommodation.'

Was no one immune to the smooth Whitney powers of persuasion? Meredith wondered bitterly. Already, he'd captured the family's imagination. Suggestions were replacing accusations, enthusiasm vanquishing suspicion.

Unnoticed, she escaped to the kitchen where only the light above the stove was on and she could hide herself in the shadows. She'd heard enough. If he was sincere, then no doubt his plans were wonderful and generous, but as usual they didn't include her. Either she was a fool or a hopeless romantic to have believed that his whispered innuendoes earlier in the attic were anything more than a well-rehearsed prelude to seduction. She felt almost ill, as though this last deception had dealt a killing blow to her heart.

Foolish woman! He'd given her so much that she hadn't had before: knowledge and a capacity for love and passion that she'd never dreamed existed in the real world. How, then, was it possible that she should feel she'd been robbed of everything that made life worthwhile?

She leaned against the kitchen counter, her head bowed. In a way, it was here in this room that it had all started, that very first night when she'd come in here to escape him and he'd followed her. Right then, he'd begun his invasion of her heart, making her wonder, as he towered over her, what might have been possible between them if things had been different. Had she unwittingly adhered to Eleanor's philosophy? Had she wished for too much and now had to pay the price for being greedy?

She closed her eyes in sudden grief. He made her ache for all the sweet, sentimental things she'd built her dreams on: for children's faces around a table; for a man whose smile, even in a crowd, seduced her and told the world that, in his eyes, she was beautiful and desirable and the only woman alive who mattered.

Not such an impossible fantasy, really—except that now those children had Tom's eyes, his engaging grin, his unruly hair. Why did she have to choose a man who didn't want to share the dream with her?

'Leave the dishes, Cinderella,' he whispered in her ear, coming up quietly behind her, and before she could escape he had her pinned against the counter in a reprise of their first evening together.

She raised her head, calling up every last ounce of will she possessed to carry her through the moment. 'Someone has to do them,' she said, congratulating herself on her magnificent control, then cringing inside to hear herself go on, 'And I seem to be remarkably well cast in the role.'

Whine a little louder, idiot! pride chastised her. Fling yourself at his feet and wail!

His hands closed on her hips and spun her around to face him. 'Why did you leave the dining-room, Meredith? Don't you approve of what I want to do?'

'I approve,' she said, a terrible, tight ache filling her chest and squeezing her lungs. 'I think it all sounds very nice.'

She was conscious of his brilliant blue eyes searching her face and knew that it was beyond her to disguise her misery. Hungrily, she stared at his mouth and wondered if, when she was old and grey, she'd still remember so vividly how his lips had felt against hers. Or was it remotely possible the memories might one day fade to bearable? She fervently hoped so.

'And what about my plans for you?' he asked, gently mocking. 'Do they sound very nice, too?'

How cruel he was. 'I know you've always felt I should get on with my life, and I'm sure you think you've done me an enormous favour by relieving me of the responsibility of taking care of——'

'Meredith darling,' he suggested, his mouth inching closer, 'do shut up.'

He was cruel and rude, too. 'I beg your pardon?'

'I said, shut up. Cinderella...' he was so close, the warmth and tenderness in his words were filtering past her parted lips to touch her frozen heart '...is not supposed to sound like a middle-aged social worker.'

Proximity was pure torture. Helpless to prevent it, she found herself leaning towards him.

He was practically kissing her. 'I'm planning to get married,' he murmured.

Her eyes, which had drifted half closed, flew open in shock.

'What do you think of that?' His hands were up to no good, sliding up her spine and pulling her hard against him, thoroughly intimate, thoroughly outrageous.

'That sounds very nice, too,' she offered weakly.

'I don't have a glass slipper, darling Meredith, but then, I'm no prince as you've already discovered. Will you settle for a ring?'

He was dangerous. Lethal. 'What do you mean?'

He sighed and stepped back a pace. 'I knew you'd make me grovel,' he said, and dropped down on one knee. 'Meredith, darling Meredith, I'm probably doing this all wrong, but it's the first time I've proposed. Will you marry me, bear my children, and live with me for better, for worse, for the rest of our lives?'

'No,' she cried, her heart breaking, tears blurring her vision, 'I can't!'

He leapt to his feet, horrified. 'Why not?'

He was a fool. How could he not know that he'd missed out the most important words? 'Because you don't believe in winter roses,' she whispered.

'I love you!' he bellowed like a wild animal in pain. 'You know I love you! Why do you suppose I came back? Why do you think I want us to have this house to ourselves? Stop playing games with me—I can't stand it!' His voice softened to a plea she was helpless to resist. 'Tell me you'll marry me, Meredith. Please!'

He wasn't perfect, but he was close enough. 'I'll marry you,' she said, the tears running down her face.

The overhead light snapped on. 'Well, thank heaven for that!' Lucille said from the doorway. 'Perhaps now we can bring in the pumpkin pie and celebrate over dessert.'

'Turn that blasted light off and go away, Lucille,' Tom roared. 'I'm not finished yet.'

Without so much as another word, she obeyed.

He dipped his head towards Meredith, drawing her close enough that, even in the dimness, she could see the sheen of tears in his eyes. 'Tell me again,' he begged. 'I need to hear you say it again.'

'I love you,' she said, 'and of course I'll marry you.'

'Thank you,' he whispered, his voice rough with emotion. 'Thank you, my darling, for teaching me what love is all about, for loving me when I couldn't even love myself.'

It was impossible, of course, but it seemed to Meredith, as his mouth settled at last on her mouth and she could feel the sure and certain beat of his heart next to her heart, that, even though a freezing Arctic wind buffeted the old house, the air was suddenly full of the scent of roses.

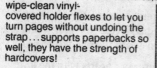